THE CREAKERS

THE CREAKERS

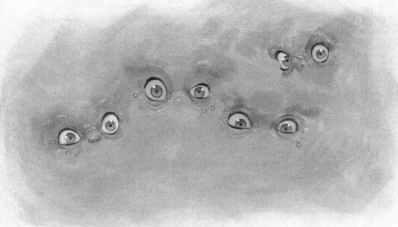

TOM FLETCHER

Illustrations by Shane Devries

Random House 🏠 New York

Cover, text, and illustrations copyright © 2017 by Tom Fletcher
Illustrations by Shane Devries

All rights reserved. Published in the United States by Random House Children's Books, a division of Penguin Random House LLC, New York. Originally published in hardcover by Penguin Random House UK, London, in 2017.

Random House and the colophon are registered trademarks of Penguin Random House LLC.

Visit us on the Web! rhcbooks.com

Educators and librarians, for a variety of teaching tools, visit us at RHTeachersLibrarians.com

Library of Congress Cataloging-in-Publication Data
Names: Fletcher, Tom, author. | Devries, Shane, illustrator.
Title: The Creakers / Tom Fletcher; illustrated by Shane Devries.
Description: First American edition. | New York: Random House, [2019] | "Originally published in hardcover by Penguin Random House UK, London, in 2017."
Summary: Searching for answers after all the adults in her town disappear, eleven-year-old Lucy goes through a passage under her bed into an upside-down world inhabited by sticky, smelly Creakers.
Identifiers: LCCN 2018050233 | ISBN 978-1-5247-7334-2 (hardcover) | ISBN 978-1-5247-7335-9 (hardcover library binding) | ISBN 978-1-5247-7336-6 (ebook)
Subjects: | CYAC: Missing persons—Fiction. | Monsters—Fiction. | Adventure and adventurers—Fiction. | Humorous stories.
Classification: LCC PZ7.F6358 Cre 2019 | DDC [Fic]—dc23

Printed in the United States of America
10 9 8 7 6 5 4 3 2 1
First American Edition

*For Giovanna, because
I haven't dedicated a book to you
yet and I feel bad. X*

You are about to have an ADVENTURE with:

Lucy Dungston

Norman Quirk

Ella Noying

Mr. Dungston
(Lucy's dad)

Mrs. Dungston
(Lucy's mom)

The Creakers

CONTENTS

What silently waits in the shadows at night?

What's under your bed, keeping just out of sight?

What's patiently waiting while you're counting sheep?

What never comes out unless you're fast asleep?

What makes all the creaks, cracks, and clangs in your house?

It isn't the cat, or your dog, or a mouse.

Those noises are made by mysterious creatures.

Read on if you dare and you might meet . . .

. . . the Creakers.

THE NIGHT IT ALL BEGAN

The sun disappeared behind the pointed silhouettes of the rooftops of Whiffington Town, like a hungry black dog swallowing a ball of flames.

A thick, eerie darkness fell like no other night Whiffington had ever known. The moon itself barely had enough courage to peek around the clouds, as though it knew that tonight something strange was going to happen.

Mothers and fathers throughout Whiffington tucked their children into bed, unaware that this would be the last bedtime story, the last good-night kiss, the last time they'd switch off the light.

Midnight.

One o'clock.

Two o'clock.

Three o'clock.

CREAK . . .

A strange noise broke the silence.

It came from inside one of the houses. With the whole town fast asleep, who could possibly have made that sound?

Or perhaps not *who* but *WHAT*?

. . . CREAK!

There it was again. This time from another house.

Creak!

Creeaak!

CREEEAAAAAK!

The Night It All Began

The sound of creaky wooden floorboards echoed around the hallways of every home in Whiffington.

Something was inside.

Something was **creaking** about.

Something not human.

There were no screams. There were no nightmares. The children slept peacefully, wonderfully unaware that the world around them had changed. It had all happened silently, as if by some strange sort of dark magic, and they wouldn't know anything about it until they woke up the next morning, on the day it all began . . .

CHAPTER ONE
THE DAY IT ALL BEGAN

L et's start on the day it all began.

On the day it all began, Lucy Dungston woke up.

Right. Well, that's a start, but it's not very exciting, is it? Let's try again.

On the day it all began, Lucy Dungston woke up to a rather unusual sound . . .

OK, that's a little better. Let's see what happens next . . .

It was the sound of the alarm clock ringing in her mom's bedroom.

Well, it's got a bit boring again, hasn't it? Let's try that bit one more time . . .

THE DAY IT ALL BEGAN

It was the sound of the alarm clock ringing in her mom's bedroom, because Lucy's mom wasn't there to switch it off. You see, Lucy was about to find out that while she was asleep in the night her mom had disappeared . . .

OH. MY. GOSH!

Imagine waking up to find that your mom has disappeared in the night! It gives me the creepy tingles every time I tell this story. I bet you're thinking, This is going to be the best scary story ever. I can't wait to read it and tell all my friends that I'm really brave because I wasn't even one bit scared.

Even though you were totally scared all the way through.

Well, this is only just the beginning. Wait until you read what happens later when the Creakers come out.

Let me know if you get scared . . . because I am!

Back on the day it all began, Lucy climbed out of bed, slipped on her fluffy blue bathrobe, and walked across her creaky floorboards, which were warm from the morning sunlight creeping in through the curtains.

Would you like to know what Lucy looked like?

THE CREAKERS

Of course you would! Here's a picture . . .

As you can see, she had shorter hair than most girls', and it was as brown as mud, or chocolate, and even though Lucy liked it to be short, her mom insisted she wear bangs.

"It stops you looking like a boy!" her mom would say (this was before she disappeared, of course). This really wound Lucy up, as her bangs always seemed to flop into her eyes, meaning she constantly had to lick her hand and slick them over to one side just so she could see.

Her eyes, once the bangs were out of the way, were greeny-brown . . . or perhaps browny-green. Either way, they were a bit green and a bit brown. You could say there was nothing particularly remarkable about Lucy at all, and it's true; she was no different from any other child in Whiffington, which is another way of saying she was quite remarkable indeed.

Anyway, more about that later.

"Mom?" Lucy called, padding across the landing toward her mom's bedroom.

But of course you already know there was no reply because her mom was gone!

Lucy's heart started beating faster in her chest as she gently opened the bedroom door and stuck her head inside.

Mrs. Dungston's book was still on the bedside table, a bookmark poking out, with her reading glasses perched on top. Her empty cocoa cup with the yellow polka-dot pattern sat beside it. Her slippers were neatly positioned on the floor. It was all as it usually was. Except for the piercing ringing of the alarm clock and the spooky empty bed.

Lucy stopped the alarm clock and ran to check the bathroom.

Empty bath.

Empty shower.

Empty toilet (although Lucy would have been very surprised to find her mom hiding there).

She ran downstairs.

Empty kitchen.

Empty living room.

Empty everywhere.

"Mom? **MOM?**" she called, a note of panic rising in her voice, and her heart leaping like a frog in her chest.

She was beginning to get an awful feeling that something terrible might have happened . . . and it was a feeling that Lucy already knew.

You see, the really creepy thing was that this wasn't the first time it had happened to Lucy Dungston.

A few months ago her dad had vanished too!

Unbelievable, right?

Lucy's mom had been devastated.

"Must have run off with another woman," Lucy had

heard one of the other moms whispering in the school playground.

"What a cheating, rotten man!" another had said, shaking her head.

But Lucy didn't think her dad was rotten at all. She couldn't believe he would run off without saying good-bye to her, without leaving a note, without saying where he was going, without finishing the half-eaten chocolate cookie and barely sipped cup of tea she'd found on his bedside table the next morning.

So on *this* morning, on the day it all began, Lucy had the strangest feeling that somehow this was all connected, that something weird was going on.

Lucy ran down the hallway, snatched the phone from the little wobbly table, and dialed her mom's phone number (which she knew by heart for emergencies, like every sensible eleven-year-old should). But as her mom's phone started ringing, Lucy saw it flashing on the arm of the sofa.

Lucy ended the call and hung her head in defeat.

Defeat . . . feet . . . shoes . . . her mom's shoes!

She ran to the front door. A pair of cozy, flat slip-ons

with flower-shaped sparkly bits was sitting on the mat, exactly where her mom kicked them off every night and where she'd slip back into them before leaving the house each day. Surely her mom wouldn't have left the house without her shoes . . . would she?

Lucy's heart sank. This all seemed far too familiar. On the day her father disappeared, one of the strangest things was that his favorite chunky black boots with the yellow laces, which he wore every single day, were still sitting by the front door, like he'd never left. Just like her mom's shoes!

Lucy knew there was only one thing to do. She was going to have to call the police.

She'd never done that before, and her heart was pounding like a drum in her chest as she dialed nine-one-one with a shaky, nervous finger.

Now what do you suppose happened next? If you think a police officer answered the phone and said, *"It's OK, Lucy, we've found your mom and we'll bring her home right away and we'll even pick up some breakfast for you too. What would you like?"* then you'd be very wrong indeed and should probably never write a book.

What actually happened was possibly the worst thing Lucy could think of . . .

Nothing.

The phone just rang, and rang, and rang, and carried on ringing until Lucy hung up.

"Since when do the police not answer the phone?" Lucy said to herself, her voice sounding unusually loud in the empty house.

A little voice in her head told her the answer: *When something spooky is going on . . .*

Lucy pulled open the front door and stepped out into the stinking morning air. Oh, it was quite normal for the air to be stinky outside the Dungston family's house. It smelled like a mixture of farts with a hint of mature sock cheese, and had a sharp after-scent of freshly brewed cabbage. It wasn't the house that smelled—it was the truck parked in the driveway. It was one of those chunky, clunky, nostril-stinging, rubbish-collecting trucks that trundle around town with those jolly-looking, grubby people in grimy overalls collecting everyone's rotten garbage.

Lucy's dad had been one of those jolly-looking,

grubby garbage-collecting people. He was the trash collector for Whiffington Town, where he lived—*sorry*, where he USED to live—before he disappeared. Since he vanished, his truck had been parked in the driveway, stinking up the whole street. Of course, Mrs. Dungston had tried to sell the truck, but no one wanted a stinky old thing like that. Even Whiffington Scrap Metal said that the odor was too strong for them to crush the truck! And so there it stayed, on Lucy's driveway.

If you ever find yourself behind one of these trucks, take a little sniff, just a little one, and you'll know what Lucy Dungston's house smelled like.

Anyway, back to the day it all began!

Out in Lucy's street, Clutter Avenue, she noticed instantly that things weren't right. Usually there was a long line of traffic clogging up the road as moms and dads took their kids to school and went to work and drove to the post office and the hairdresser's and did all the boring stuff grown-ups do. But today the road wasn't busy. It wasn't just not-busy—it was completely deserted. Not a single car. Lucy looked left, then right, then left again, then right again, then she repeated that about twenty more times, which I won't bother to write because that would just be silly, but when she had finished she was convinced she was right—something weird was definitely happening in Whiffington Town.

"What the jiggins is going on?" she said to herself.

What the jiggins indeed, Lucy.

Where was Mr. Ratcliffe, the wrinkly old man who did yoga in his front yard in his underpants? (He claimed it was the secret to staying young.)

Where was Molly, the milk woman, who delivered fresh bottles of milk from her electric van?

Where was Mario, the man from the next street, who jogged past every morning in his skimpy Lycra shorts?

Where *was* everyone?!

That's when Lucy heard a noise. Her heart leapt. Was it her mom?

A long, slow creak came from somewhere along Clutter Avenue, followed by a sudden **CLANG!**

"Hello?" Lucy called.

"Mama?" a small voice asked from behind the fence two doors down.

"Oh, Ella! It's just you!"

Lucy sighed in relief as Ella Noying appeared. First her bouncy hair peeped out into the street, followed by her round cheeks and her big deep-brown eyes that always managed to get her out of trouble. She was wearing bright pink pajamas made of shiny silk, with her initials embroidered on the pocket. In one hand was a pair of pink heart-shaped designer sunglasses. Lucy never saw Ella anywhere without those.

"Lucy, I can't find Mama or Papa and my avocado needs mashing," Ella whined.

Before Lucy could reply, another door opened across the street.

"Dad?" whispered Norman Quirk, a boy from Lucy's year at school, as he hesitantly stepped into his front yard. Norman was dressed in a pristinely ironed, meticulously clean Scout uniform, which was covered

THE DAY IT ALL BEGAN

in the most achievement badges Lucy had ever seen.

Here is a list of some of Norman's badges:

- a *tree-climbing* badge
- a *tent-pitching* badge
- a badge for *spreading-butter-on-toast-all-the-way-to-the-edges*
- the *indoor-challenge* badge
- the *outdoor-challenge* badge
- the *shake-it-all-about-door challenge* badge
- a *bed-making* badge
- a *cake-baking* badge
- an *eating-the-cake-you-bake-in-the-bed-you-make* badge
- the *remembering-to-wash-your-belly-button* badge
- and even a badge for *collecting-lots-of-badges*

. . . and there were a few empty spots on his uniform that he needed to fill with new badges.

"Oh, hi . . . Er, I mean, good morning, civilians!"

Norman said, nervously holding up three fingers in a Scout salute before fiddling with his neatly combed mousy-blond hair. With his other hand, he covered his mouth to hide his train-track braces.

"You haven't seen my dad, have you?" he asked, scooping a handful of mud from his front yard and sniffing it as if trying to pick up his dad's scent. When Norman bent down, Lucy caught sight of his Transformers socks.

Ella giggled at him, not really in a mean way, but just because she found Norman sort of funny. Everyone did. Norman was . . . different.

Sometimes people who are different get laughed at, but it's always the different ones who make a difference, Lucy heard her dad's voice say in her head. He had his own way of looking at things. On cloudy days, he'd tell Lucy, "The sun just needs a holiday so it can shine better tomorrow!" When she came in second to her friend Giorgina in the sack race on Sports Day, he told her, "Don't be upset. You just made your friend really happy!" And when she asked him if he liked being a trash collector, he said, "You'd be surprised what people throw away, Lucy. One man's garbage is another man's favorite pair of black boots!" and clipped his heels together with a wink.

"No, I've not seen your dad, sorry," Lucy said, shaking off her daydream about her own father and elbowing Ella to stop her laughing. "My mom's missing too."

Suddenly another door opened and Sissy McNab ran out into the street in tears. Then Toby Cobblesmith, who had his shoes on the wrong feet. Next out came William Trundle and Brenda Payne, searching for their mom and dad, then another kid, and another, until, one by one, every child in Whiffington Town came stumbling out of their houses in their pj's, robes, and slippers, trying to find their parents. Grandmas and granddads, aunts and uncles—they were all gone too. There wasn't a single grown-up to be seen.

There was such a kerfuffle in Clutter Avenue: some children were crying; others were laughing; and a few were still fast asleep in bed and hadn't noticed anything yet.

"What's going on?" they shouted (the ones who were awake).

"Where are our parents?" they called.

17

"What are we going to do?" they yelled.

Lucy took a breath and tried to think. "What would my mom do?" she said to herself. "How did my mom find out what was going on in the world?"

Then, before she knew what she was doing, Lucy found herself clambering onto the steps of her dad's stinking garbage truck, and above the noise she yelled . . .

"THE NEWS!"

There was silence. Everyone turned to look at Lucy.

"We have to watch the news! I know it's super-boring, but whenever my mom wants to know what's going on in the world she always watches the news," she told them.

The children looked at each other, uncertain. I'm sure you know that the news is the biggest snorefest on TV, but Lucy had a point.

"She's right . . . ," Norman whispered to Ella, too frightened to say it out loud.

"SHE'S RIGHT!" Ella shouted, not frightened of anyone.

"To the television!" they all cried in unison, and every

18

THE DAY IT ALL BEGAN

child on Clutter Avenue in Whiffington Town pushed past Lucy and piled into her house.

In a matter of seconds her living room was full from carpet to ceiling with scared children in their pj's. There were children sitting on the floor. There were children sitting on the children sitting on the floor.

There were even children sitting on the children sitting on the children sitting on the floor! They were all terrified, mainly because their parents were missing, but also a little bit freaked out because they were about to watch the news without being made to.

Lucy switched on her TV.

"Have you got any popcorn?" asked a child sitting on the floor.

"Sorry, I don't think we do," Lucy replied.

"Chocolate cookies?" asked a child sitting on the child sitting on the floor.

"No chocolate cookies either. Mom doesn't buy those anymore. Not since—well, never mind. We just don't have any."

"You mean we have to watch TV without any snacks?" moaned Ella, who was sitting on the child sitting on the child sitting on the floor.

"Oh, OK—I'll see what we've got!" promised Lucy, whizzing off to the kitchen. She returned a few minutes later with all the boxes of cereal from the cupboard and handed them around the room. "Take a handful and pass it on," she said, then got back to finding the twenty-four-hour news channel.

The moment it flicked on, her heart stopped.

"Oh no!" Lucy cried. **"Look!"**

The crowd of children all spat out their cornflakes and Cheerios in shock, showering the room with chewed bits of soggy cereal.

On the TV they could see the normal news desk, the normal sheets of paper, and the normal coffee mug, but there was something very *not*-normal about it.

The news presenter was missing!

Ella pushed through to the front. "Try another channel! Maybe your TV is broken, Lucy. Don't you have a *TV-repair* badge?" she demanded, turning to Norman, who tried his best to hide when everyone looked at him.

"Perhaps I could take a look?" he said sheepishly as the children nudged him across the room toward the TV. "Sorry, oops, watch out!" he muttered as he stepped on almost everybody's fingers.

"Well? Why isn't it working?" Ella said, bashing the remote on the side of the TV.

"Erm . . . well . . . I actually *do* have a badge in *TV-remote-control functions*. And as the only member of the Whiffington Scout Troop present today—"

"Aren't you the *only* member of the Scout troop, full stop?" asked Ella. Everybody laughed.

Looking defeated, Norman sat down on what he thought was the arm of the sofa, but it was actually the head of another child sitting on another child.

"Here, just do your best," Lucy said, taking the remote from Ella and handing it to Norman. Norman smiled at her, for once forgetting to hide his braces. He flicked through a few channels, hoping to find a grown-up of any kind looking back out at them.

Silly Sunrise, the kids' show, had no Funzo the Clown getting pied in the face today. *Wakey-Wakey, Whiffington* had no Piers Snoregan, although that was probably an improvement. Norman flicked through the sports channels, the shopping network, the cooking shows, Whiffington Weather, and just about every channel he could think of. Not a single one of them had a single grown-up.

THE DAY IT ALL BEGAN

It was almost as if every adult on the planet had just disappeared overnight, from Lucy's mom to the news presenter . . .

They had all just **GONE!**

OK, this isn't the next chapter, but I just wanted to check you were all right. I know it's a bit spooky, but trust me, it all works out in the end. At least I think it does. Maybe. Actually, I can't quite remember what happens. It might get really, REALLY scary . . . I guess we'll just have to keep going to find out.

Good luck . . .

CHAPTER TWO
THE GOODBYE NOTE

The children all looked at Lucy, waiting to be told what they should do next. And wondering if she had any more cereal.

"I wish I had an answer for you all!" Lucy said apologetically. "And more cereal. But I'm afraid I have no idea what to do—and you've eaten all the snacks I've got!"

A bunch of little kids started crying. Some of the older kids cried too. (They asked me not to write that in this book but I'm going to anyway, just so you know how bad it was. Wouldn't *you* cry if there was no more cereal left? Especially on the day your mom or dad went missing.)

Think, Lucy, think! Lucy thought to herself. *I'm trying to think, but you keep talking,* Lucy thought back. Her mind was quiet for a moment, but all she could think of was how much she wished they taught you at school what to do if you ever woke up and discovered that your mom had disappeared. That would be far more useful than the six times table!

"That's it!" Lucy shouted suddenly, making half the room jump.

"What's *it*?" replied Norman as he unpacked a camping stove from his satchel and started preparing a full breakfast.

"*School,* of course!" Lucy cried.

Everyone looked at her as if she'd lost it.

"We need to go to *school,*" she repeated.

"First you *want* to watch the news, now you *want* to go to school . . . What sort of kid are you?" Ella asked, slipping on her heart-shaped sunglasses even though she was inside, like some sort of Whiffington celebrity.

"The kind who wants to find out what's going on and get our parents back! I've tried the police. We've tried the television. Now there's only one place left—school!" said Lucy.

The crowd of watching children blinked in unison. No one really *wanted* to go to school, but once again Lucy had a point.

"Right, I'm off. Who's coming with me?" Lucy said hopefully.

There was a very unenthusiastic mumble from the other kids.

"Yeah, all right."

"S'pose so."

"If we *have* to . . ."

"Are you sure there's no more cereal?"

"But my eggs aren't poached yet," said Norman, looking at his stopwatch.

Lucy ignored them all and climbed over their heads and disappeared out of the room. A few moments later she bounded back in wearing her school uniform, looking ready for a normal school day.

"What are you wearing that for?" scoffed Ella, peeping over her shades.

"If the teachers are at school, then I can't show up in

my bathrobe and expect them to take me seriously," Lucy said. She felt her cheeks flushing hot with embarrassment as the room stared at her. But Lucy wasn't the sort of kid who skipped school. Nor did she turn up to class wearing her nightwear. She liked lessons and learning.

"A kid who wants to be smart is already a smart kid," Lucy said. "My dad told me that once."

With that, Lucy picked up her school bag, flung it over her shoulder, and bounded out of her front door, pretending not to give a hoot about the other children.

She began marching up the street toward Whiffington School, along the road that was usually full of cars. As it was now empty, she decided she'd walk down the middle of the road. It was an eerie sensation.

She walked past Old Man Carvey's Butcher Shop— **CLOSED.**

She walked past Whiffington Library—**CLOSED.**

She walked past Scrummy McScroodles Sweets 'n' Stuff—**CLOSED! CLOSED!! CLOSED!!!**

Whiffington was a ghost town.

Suddenly Lucy heard footsteps behind her. She

29

whipped around, and to her surprise she saw the crowd of children from her living room following her down the middle of the street. More children were following them, others were jogging up the pavement, and kids had started filing out of their houses.

"There she is," Lucy heard children whisper.

"The girl who wants to go to school."

"She knows what to do!"

"She's the one in charge."

In charge? Lucy thought. *Why on earth am* I *in charge?*

But before she could question it, the bunch of kids closest to her started nudging her along, forcing her to keep going, to lead them all to the school.

"What the jiggins?" Lucy said. "Hang on just a sec!"

And at that the children stopped.

"First of all, I am *not* in charge," Lucy said.

The children stood still, waiting to hear a *second of all* . . .

"Second of all . . ."

Lucy hadn't thought of a *second of all* yet. "Erm . . . Second of all, we're already late, so we'd better get a move on!" She licked her hand, slicked her bangs over to one side, and marched on toward the school with her new army of children still in their pj's and slippers following closely behind, some of the little ones even dragging their favorite teddy along for the adventure. Lucy suddenly felt a sense of achievement. They were taking control. Things were about to get better.

Or so she thought.

The muffled sound of fluffy slippers stomping over the pavement filled the air as they walked toward the school. Surely there would be a grown-up there who could help.

But when they arrived at the large iron gates of Whiffington School, Lucy stopped dead in her tracks, causing everyone to bump into each other behind her.

"I'm really sorry that you all followed me here, but the school gates are locked!" Lucy said, lifting up the big metal padlock so that everyone could see. Then she peered through the bars of the gates, looking for any sign of life inside. But the windows of the school were dark and cold. No grown-ups were in there today.

Lucy gulped as hundreds of faces stared disappointedly at her.

"So now what do we do?" a little voice cried out.

"I don't know," replied Lucy, feeling awful that she'd let everyone down.

"If only I had a pin. I've got my *lock-picking* badge, you know," said Norman, proudly pointing at it.

"Where have all the grown-ups gone?" Ella whined.

"I don't know that either," said Lucy.

"I believe they may have gone due east," said Norman, checking his compass against the position of the sun.

"Why is this happening?" the children cried.

"I DON'T KNOW!" Lucy yelled, feeling a lump rise in her throat. "I don't know what's happening, why it's happening, where the grown-ups have gone, or when they're coming back. I just woke up like everyone else and found that my mom was missing—that's all! I don't have the answers. I'm just a kid like you!"

Everyone let out a long, disappointed sigh. The younger kids hugged their teddy bears as their bottom lips started trembling. They had all hoped that Lucy would be like one of those super-smart kids they'd all seen in the movies—you know, those movies where things go wrong and somehow there's always one kid who knows how to sort it all out.

What they didn't realize was that Lucy Dungston definitely *was* one of those kids.

She just didn't know it yet.

34

"You might as well all go home and wait there. It's probably the safest thing to do," Lucy said.

Slowly the children started to leave. They hung their heads and dragged their feet in the dirt as they wandered back through the empty streets to their empty houses.

Lucy rested her head on the cold gates. *No Mom, no police, no teachers, no cereal. This is bad,* she thought.

She was just about to start trudging home herself when a gust of wind blew past her face, causing her to turn away. It whooshed over the playground and toward the front door of the school.

Sometimes the wind gusts in just the right place, at just the right time, blowing you in the right direction.

That's when Lucy saw it, flapping in the breeze like a hand waving at her. It was a piece of paper pinned to the front door of the school.

Her heart stopped.

"Wait!" she cried, and all the children stopped in their tracks and turned back. "Look!" she added, pointing at the piece of paper on the door.

Without thinking, Lucy started climbing one of the large iron gates. Just as her fingers gripped the top, her foot slipped through the gap between the metal bars. She managed to cling on tight with her hands, but her feet dangled uselessly beneath her, swinging this way and that, unable to find a foothold.

Everyone gasped.

Then, all of a sudden, Norman did the strangest thing. He ran over to Lucy and crouched down underneath her on all fours, like some sort of dog.

"What—are—you—doing?!" Lucy strained as she gripped the top of the gate.

"Someone needs to get on my back," Norman said, so quietly that hardly anyone heard him.

"SOMEONE GET ON HIS BACK!"

Ella blasted.

The kids suddenly realized what Norman was trying to do—make a human pyramid! Quickly, two older girls from the hockey team crouched on the ground next to him, and a couple more kids climbed onto *their* backs. Finally the tips of Lucy's toes brushed against someone's bottom, and she could step on them, completing the pyramid.

"Thanks!" Lucy said as she swung her legs over the

gate with ease, dropped down into
the empty playground, and ran
toward the small piece of paper
that was pinned to the door.
She reached up, plucked out
the pin, and took the paper
down. Her hands shook with
nerves as she flipped it
over, inspecting it.

It was a letter, and judging by the writing on the front, it was meant for them.

As she looked more closely at the dirty brown writing, she began to worry about what this letter might say. Something about the word on the front suddenly seemed frightening.

Childrun

Perhaps it was the way it glistened in the sunlight: not in a nice way, but in a horrid, sticky sort of way.

"Pass me the pin!" Norman said, stretching his open hand through the gates.

Lucy handed it to him and he set to work picking the lock. After a few seconds of fiddly fingerwork, Norman had the school gates open, so that Lucy could rejoin the rest of the children. "Told you," he said to Ella with a braces-revealing grin as he proudly rubbed his *lock-picking* badge.

"Read it, Lucy!" cried Ella.

With a trembling hand, Lucy straightened the paper and took a deep breath.

"What does it say?" Norman asked, pulling a pair of reading glasses out of his Scout uniform pocket.

In the same dirty brown writing was this:

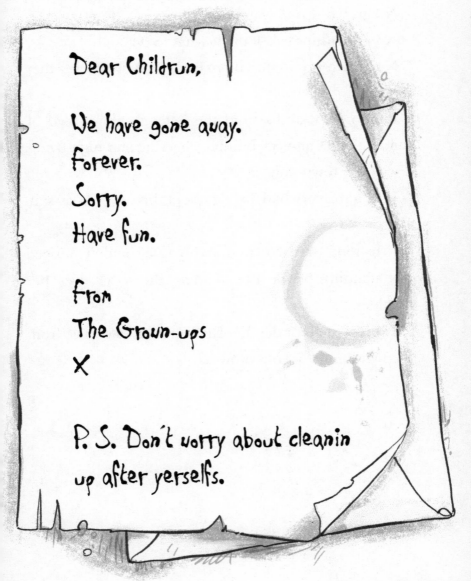

Dear Childrun,

We have gone away.
Forever.
Sorry.
Have fun.

From
The Groun-ups
X

P. S. Don't worry about cleanin up after yerselfs.

Everyone was silent. The grown-ups had gone away. Forever.

The children were alone.

No grown-ups to watch over them.

No grown-ups to tell them what to do.

No grown-ups to stop them from doing whatever they wanted.

Lucy nervously lowered the letter as the crowd of children burst into celebration, cheering and high-fiving. It was *their* town now!

"I've got a very bad feeling about this . . . ," Lucy said to herself.

"Me too," said Norman, who Lucy hadn't noticed was standing beside her, reading the letter over her shoulder.

"This is the best day EV-ER!" cried Ella's voice from deep within the joyous crowd.

You see, that chapter wasn't scary, was it? Imagine a world where there were no grown-ups telling you, "Don't eat twelve chocolate bars!" and "Don't sit so close to the TV" and "Don't climb out of the window of that four-story building" . . . Just imagine that! What would you get up to if there were no grown-ups around? Oooh, this will make a good chapter! Let's see what Lucy did.

CHAPTER THREE
HELPFUL

Lucy went home and did her homework.

Oh, Lucy, you're such a boring snorebag!

"No, I'm not!" said Lucy.

Yes, you are! These people didn't buy this book to read about you doing your homework! This book is all about how you save the town!

"Is it?" Lucy asked.

Yes! Now put that homework down and go and get on with it!

Lucy put her homework down and went and got on with it.

First she changed out of her school uniform and got into her favorite denim overalls.

"Well, if I'm not going to school, I might as well be comfortable," she said to herself, clipping up the buttons and suddenly feeling nice and comfy and ready to get stuff done. Funny how overalls do that.

"That's better," she said, licking her hand and slicking her bangs over to one side.

Just as she did this . . .

CRAAAASSSHH!

Lucy ran outside to see a car sticking out of her mom's neat hedge in the front yard. Steam and smoke were hissing out of the engine, and she could hear laughter and giggles coming from inside.

"What the jiggins?" Lucy cried as the driver's door swung open and she saw the person behind the wheel. Actually, it was two people: two young boys from her school. They were brothers and always getting into trouble.

"Buzz? Buddy?" Lucy cried. "What on earth are you doing?"

Buzz was sitting at the steering wheel, barely able to see out of the window, while Buddy was crouched on the floor, operating the pedals.

"Just going for a spin," Buzz explained.

"But you're a little boy! You can't drive!"

Buddy called out from under the steering wheel, "Why have we stopped?"

"I think we're out of gas!" Buzz replied.

"You've stopped because you've crashed, you nitwits, and you're lucky you didn't hurt anyone, or yourselves!" Lucy cried. "Now get out of that car, or I'm going to tell . . ." She paused.

The boys looked up at her.

"Who?" asked Buzz, and the boys smiled with the cheeky smile people use when they know they can get away with something.

"Oh!" said Lucy, suddenly realizing that there was absolutely nobody she could tell. Nobody to stop these boys from doing whatever they wanted.

She was on her own.

"Well, children can't drive around in cars. It's silly and dangerous," said Lucy, and she reached into the car through the open door, switched off the engine, and took away the keys.

"Hey, those are our dad's keys!" Buzz said. "You can't take those! It's stealing!"

"Exactly, they're your *dad's* keys for your *dad's* car. What would he say if he saw you both now?" Lucy said.

"Yeah, but he *can't* see us, can he?" replied Buzz.

"But he will when he comes back. Unless you think

your dad is never coming back. Do you?" Lucy said.

Buzz's face changed suddenly.

"Course he's coming back!" Buddy insisted.

"Good, and when he does, you can tell him to come and pick his keys up from me. Until then, I'll look after them." And with that, Lucy popped the keys in the pocket of her overalls.

She was just about to head back inside when she heard someone calling her name from farther up the street.

"Lucy! Lucy! I need your help!"

Lucy followed the faint cries to Ella's front door and walked inside. Ella had got herself wedged inside the washing machine while playing hide-and-seek. To be fair, she hadn't been found for three hours, and by that point no one else was playing the game, so technically she had won.

"Yes! I'm the best!" Ella cheered as Lucy carefully removed the door with a screwdriver, like she'd seen her dad do once, and Ella was free to continue annoying her friends.

"Right, time for a sandwich!" Lucy said to herself, rubbing her hungry tummy, but . . .

"Lucy! Help!" another voice called out.

Lucy sighed and quickly headed in the direction of the child in need. By the time she'd helped that one, there was another, then another, and another—followed by even more!

On that day—the day it all began—
twelve separate kids got their hands stuck
in cookie jars. Seven got Play-Doh wedged
up their nostrils. One managed to paint
herself purple . . . even in her belly button!

And every single child wanted Lucy to
help them out.

Lucy's afternoon continued like this until long after the sun had set. She ended up helping half the population of Whiffington, and by the end of that day you wouldn't believe the state of the town itself.

What do you mean, *you would*?

OK—check this out.

The houses were so messy they looked like they'd been decorated for Halloween. Toilet paper hung from the branches of every tree, windows were flung wide open, and sofas had been shoved out into front yards, with children jumping on them.

WITH THEIR SHOES ON!

One house had the entire contents of its living room spread out on the roof, and another had the entire roof in the living room. It was as though all of Whiffington had turned completely topsy-turvy! The grown-ups hadn't even been gone for twenty-four hours yet, and already the town looked like a scene from a disaster movie.

As she walked home that evening, Lucy helped anyone who needed it and picked up as much trash as she could, dumping it in the back of her dad's truck. Being responsible had become part of who Lucy was, especially since her dad left. She'd seen how tough it was for her mom, and she'd had to grow up pretty quickly.

So, while all the other kids spent this first grown-up-free night causing mayhem and getting up to mischief, staying up late, eating ice cream for dinner and pizza-burgers for dessert (pizza-burgers are burgers stuffed inside two slices of pizza instead of burger buns; they're amazing—you should try them if your parents ever go missing), Lucy was getting herself ready for bed. She was the only child in Whiffington to brush their teeth that night. She was also the only child in Whiffington to wash the dishes, take the garbage out, put on pj's, read a bedtime story, and turn out the light.

Just as she was getting all cozy on her pillow, a great racket broke the silence.

"Lucy, can we have our dad's car keys back, please?" called up Buzz from outside. His voice was loud and echoey, and when Lucy peered out of the window, she saw that he was using a megaphone. "We promise we won't drive it."

"But I thought you said we were going to break the

land-speed record?" whispered Buddy, his voice amplified by the megaphone.

"Shhhhh!" hissed Buzz.

Lucy slipped downstairs, stuck her hand out of the front door, and quickly took the megaphone from the noisy boys. She tucked it into a safe hiding place along with their father's car keys: inside the fridge.

All was quiet, and Lucy was exhausted. She walked back up the stairs to her bedroom and climbed under the covers.

"Peace at last!" she sighed.

What Lucy didn't realize was that, even though her mom and dad weren't there, she wasn't alone.

There was someone else in Lucy's house.

There was some*thing* else in Lucy's room.

Something hiding under Lucy's bed, waiting for her to fall asleep—just like it did every night . . .

OK, so things are about to get a little scary. Don't say I didn't warn you. Are you ready? Take a deep breath.

Here we go . . .

Chapter Four
LUCY WASN'T ALONE

Lucy's eyelids were feeling heavy. She was exhausted after her busy day helping the kids of Whiffington adjust to life with no grown-ups about. However, even though she felt more tired than she'd ever been, for some reason she couldn't sleep.

She lay on her bed and started to imagine she was sinking peacefully into the mattress, as if it were a fluffy cloud. She closed her eyes, and for a moment she could see her mom perched on the edge of her bed, where Mrs. Dungston normally sat each night. Lucy's mom would slip off the hairband holding her hair back, letting her long brown curls fall down past her shoulders as she sipped on their nightly shared mug of cocoa before handing it to Lucy.

"Close your eyes, my little Lucypops," Mrs. Dungston would say, her brown eyes twinkling. "Feel yourself floating on the fluffiest cloud. Light as a feather."

"But, Mom, I'm too awake to go to sleep. It's impossible!" Lucy would answer.

"Impossible isn't real, Lucypops. It's just in your mind."

Lucy felt the corners of her mouth rise into a little smile at her mom's nickname for her—Lucypops. Her dad used to call her this too. Before he left.

Suddenly the fluffy cloud she was floating on in her mind dissolved, and she was just lying on her cold mattress in her empty room in her empty house. Alone.

Impossible certainly felt very real.

She quickly closed her eyes again in an attempt to get back on that cozy cloud. She tried to imagine her body sinking into it. It was her favorite thing to imagine. But on the night of the day it all began, Lucy's mind just couldn't imagine things right. Her comfy cloud was not as comfy without her mom there.

Where are you, Mom? Lucy thought as she rolled onto

her side and looked at the full moon through the gap in the curtains as it watched over Whiffington Town. Was her mom out there somewhere?

Lucy tried to shake the worry out of her head. She rolled this way and that, then that way and this. But neither way was working, so she just settled on her back, staring up at the ceiling. Her heart sank as the little glow-in-the-dark stars and planets looked back down at her: her dad had once arranged them into a giant smiley face on the ceiling.

Lucy Wasn't Alone

Lucy realized that there were reminders of her parents dotted all over her room. Out of the corner of her eye she could see the certificate presented by her dad on the day she broke the family jelly bean–eating record, gulping down twenty-seven in thirty seconds. (Even the green ones.) She turned away from the wall, but this put her face to face with the bookcase, which was overflowing with all the stories her mom read with her.

The absence of her mom made it very quiet in her house. Unusually quiet. So quiet, in fact, that the silence was almost loud. Lucy tried humming a little song to herself, a lullaby, but it didn't help. It just reminded her of her dad.

"Time for a song, Lucypops," she pictured him saying as he reached into his pocket for his most prized possession: his silver harmonica. "Any requests?" he always asked, but Lucy knew he was teasing, because he always played the same song. It was one he had written himself, and it was called "Lucy's Lullaby." He'd played it to her every night until he disappeared.

Lucy sighed.

She got out of bed and walked over to her wardrobe, but just as she was about to open the door she heard a tiny noise. It sounded like the creak of her floorboards.

Lucy suddenly felt a little chill, a shiver running down her back, like someone was watching her (which you already know was true, but Lucy didn't yet).

"Hello?" she called.

She looked over her shoulder, but there was no one there.

Lucy Wasn't Alone

"Don't be such a silly sausage, Lucy," she whispered firmly to herself. "You're just getting the chills because you're alone. Now, pull yourself together."

With that, she opened her wardrobe and lifted a wooden panel on the floor, which revealed a secret hiding place. This was where she kept special things she didn't want anyone else to find.

There wasn't much in it. A pretty shell she'd found at the beach once. A smashed-up pebble that had gotten her to second place in the playground hopscotch championships. And a framed photograph.

She picked it up and stared at it. Three people smiled up at her from the picture: a young Lucy with her arms wrapped around her mother's neck as she kissed Lucy on the head and, behind them both, cradling the two most precious things in his life in his arms, Lucy's dad.

Lucy's heart ached every time she looked at this photo, at how happy the three of them were. She always made an extra effort to study her dad's face, as if she was afraid that somehow she might forget him. She held the photo close so she could see every detail.

She saw his eyes, which were a deep, twinkling blue.

His nose, which was a little bit big, just like hers.

His mouth, which looked like it might break into a smile and make the dimple in his cheek appear at any moment.

She smiled to herself and hugged the photo to her chest.

There was one more thing hidden in Lucy's secret hiding place, folded neatly underneath the other treasures. It was a bright fluorescent-green color and was giving off an awful stench of stewed sprouts and fish scales. Lucy pulled out her dad's stinking work coat, the one he had worn when he was driving the big smelly garbage truck. She'd kept it hidden in here so her mom wouldn't find it and throw it away, like the rest of her dad's stuff.

Lucy slid her arms into the sleeves and put on the bright, smelly jacket. It was far too big and engulfed her like a stinky fluorescent duvet. She sat down, her back against her wardrobe, and took a deep breath. The disgusting fumes filled her nostrils with comforting memories of her dad, and she suddenly felt a little better.

She snuggled into the coat and made herself comfy

on the floor, but as she wriggled, something fell out of its pocket and clunked loudly on the floorboards. Something silver and shiny.

It was her dad's harmonica.

She picked it up, smiling, and played "Lucy's Lullaby" as best she could. It wasn't as magical as when her dad played it, but it melted away some of her troubles, at least for a moment.

When she finished, she held it tight in her hands and stared at the reflection on its shiny surface. She saw her face looking back at her. Then she tilted it slightly and saw the moon through the curtains. A little more, and she saw her bedside table, then her bed, and then the beady black eyes of the creature hiding under it . . .

WHAT?!

The Creakers

Lucy looked up from the harmonica and stared into the blackness of the shadowy gap beneath her bed, but the watching eyes had gone.

Her heart was racing—no, *sprinting*—in her chest. Had she imagined it? Or had there *really* been a pair of shiny eyes looking at her from underneath the bed?

Lucy wanted to stand up, but she couldn't. She was frozen to the spot, frozen with fear. She was completely on her own in her dark bedroom, in her quiet house, in the middle of the night, with a creature lurking under her bed.

And things were about to get even weirder . . .

Chapter Five
THE FIRST CREAKER

Have you ever been so scared that you couldn't move? So utterly terrified that you're just frozen, helplessly waiting for something nasty to come and get you in the night? Praying for the sun to come up and make everything OK again?

That's how Lucy was feeling.

She was sitting on her bedroom floor, trembling with fear, wrapped in her dad's stinky garbage-collecting coat, her sweat-soaked hair sticking to her forehead and her heart beating like a drum in her chest, and she was completely unable to move. Paralyzed with fear.

She tried to say *Hello?* But she barely even managed

the *H,* let alone the *ello*! So she just sat there, staring into the shadows beneath her bed where she'd seen those two dark eyes watching her.

She couldn't tell how long she stayed frozen—minutes, hours? Time doesn't seem to exist when you're that scared. However long it was, after what felt like forever of staring into the darkness, somehow Lucy drifted off to sleep.

Now, I know what you're thinking: *How can you fall asleep if you're that scared?* Well, *that's* just the thing . . . You can't!

Not unless a Creaker is there.

What's a Creaker? Don't tell me you've never heard of the Creakers!

Well, it's the name of this book, for starters. Haven't you been paying any attention?

Have you ever heard noises in your house when you're in bed at night? *That* is a Creaker.

Have you ever felt as though there's something else with you in your bedroom? *That's* a Creaker too.

Have you ever found a sack of presents by the fireplace on Christmas Day? *Wait,* that's not a Creaker—that's Santa.

The First Creaker

Have you ever managed to fall asleep, even when you were so scared it seemed impossible? That's definitely a Creaker! It's one of their naughty little tricks, and that's exactly what this creepy little Creaker used on Lucy that night.

She didn't notice anything at all, but from under the bed came a gust of hot air. It was the reeking breath of the Creaker as he blew a clawful of something golden and crumbly into her bedroom, which silently drifted into her eyes and settled there without Lucy suspecting a thing.

Ten minutes later she was fast a-snooze, leaving the Creaker to creep out of his hiding place.

In his bedroom on the other side of Clutter Avenue, Norman Quirk was in his favorite Transformers pj's, busy ironing.

"Creases, creases, creases!" he huffed as he ran the hot iron over his Scout uniform for the fifth time that night. The pants were always the hardest part, and without his dad there to help he just couldn't get them as neatly pressed as he thought was acceptable for a young Scout.

"Hmph, I'm afraid that'll have to do." He sighed, shaking his tired head as he examined each pant leg through his magnifying glass. He slid them onto a hanger, which he hung on the silver handle of his wardrobe door, ready for the morning.

Creak.

Norman froze. The noise had come from behind him. Then he noticed, in the polished surface of the wardrobe door handle, two little black specks like beady eyes staring at him from under his bed.

"Hello?" he whispered, terrified of what might be lurking behind him.

There was no reply. He swallowed his fear, gripped

the iron, and whipped around in a flash, but there was nothing. No beady black eyes. Just shelves lined with his Transformers collection.

He sighed in relief, his heart pounding.

"At least I've got you here for company!" he said as he dropped some food into the fish tank for his two pet underwater snails. (Norman used to have a goldfish, but it ran away—at least that's what his dad told him.) He watched as what looked like two boogers wearing shells slowly slurped up the side of the tank, their oily dark green bodies leaving a trail on the inside of the glass.

He yawned and reached into the cold water to pat each snail on its hard, slimy shell.

"Good night, Optimus. Good night, Megatron," he said, then he grabbed his flashlight from the table, switched off his bedroom light, and leapt into bed.

He stayed up for a while reading. He read a page of *Scout Monthly*, learning the latest knot-tying techniques. It was his favorite thing to read before bed, but as he turned to the next page, he suddenly felt as though a cloud of tiredness had fallen over him. He shook his head, rubbed his eyes, and began reading the first line when . . .

CREAK!

"H-hello?" Norman croaked, now feeling weak and floppy. He was sure he'd heard someone in his room, but sleep was just . . . too . . . tempting.

His eyes closed automatically and his head fell back onto his fluffy pillow as he drifted into a strange dream about slimy green creatures with oily skin making creaking noises under his bed.

*

Lucy skipped along the street in her baggy blue overalls, dragging a black plastic sack behind her.

"Dad, you forgot this one!" she called over the sound of the garbage truck starting up.

"Ah, well done, Lucypops!" Mr. Dungston said, cutting the engine and stepping out of his enormous vehicle. "Are you coming to work with me today?"

He held out his hands as Lucy struggled to lift the heavy bag off the ground. "What the jiggins have you got in there?" he said, giving her a hand.

"Just trash," Lucy said.

"Just trash?" Mr. Dungston echoed in disbelief. "*JUST* trash? My little Lucypops, it's far more than *just trash*! It's glorious, wonderful, stinking, rotten trash!" He lifted Lucy and the trash bag and spun them around. "And it's this wonderfully stinky stuff that puts food on our backs and clothes on the table."

Lucy laughed.

"Dad, you mean, *clothes on our backs and food on the table*!"

"Do I? Oh yes, I suppose I do," he teased. "Right, throw it in, then." He lifted Lucy up high so she could drop the bag of garbage into the back of the truck.

"Lovely throw, my Lucypops. Now off you trot back to your mom, and I'll see if I can turn that bag of trash into a nice roast for dinner."

He popped Lucy back on the ground, pushed her bangs to one side, and kissed her forehead before she turned and ran to her mom, who was standing in the doorway.

"Have a good day, Larry!" Mrs. Dungston called.

"Full of rotten goodness as always, my dear," he said as he swung himself up into his truck and slammed the door shut with a . . .

The First Creaker

BANG!

Lucy woke up from her dream in a startled panic.

How did I fall asleep?! she asked herself, and quickly looked around. There was an orange glow from her window as the first bit of sunlight poked through the curtains and began filling her room. The last thing she remembered was staring into the shadows beneath her bed, and the next moment she was waking up!

She blinked and felt something in the corners of her eyes. She rubbed them, and tiny clumps of sleep fell out.

Lucy wasn't sure why, but now that the sun had come up she wasn't as scared anymore. Funny how sunlight does that, isn't it? You can be scared stiff during the night, but as soon as it's daytime you feel fine again. Like we all somehow know that strange things only happen at night.

Lucy stood up, took off her dad's grubby coat,

71

returned it to its hiding place, and opened the curtains, allowing the sunlight to fill her room to the brim.

Then she lay flat on the bed and carefully lowered her head over the edge to get a good look underneath. There was a nice gap under her bed, big enough for Lucy to fit if she ever wanted to. Big enough for her to be able to see right to the other side. To her relief, there was nothing there. No scary little eyes staring back at her, just her creaky old floorboards gathering dust.

She sighed a big fat sigh.

I must have imagined it, she thought.

Was it all in my head? she wondered.

Must have been a nightmare, she hoped. *A very realistic nightmare!*

But very soon Lucy was going to find out that it *wasn't* all in her head. Before long, Lucy was going to see those little black eyes again . . . and next time the Creaker would not be alone.

Blimey! How are you doing? That was a bit intense, wasn't it? Eyes under the bed. Creaks in the dark! Well, I wish I could tell you that it all gets better from here, that the rest of the book is full of pretty winged ponies galloping across rainbows, scattering jelly beans from their hooves as they fly, but I'm afraid it isn't. It only gets worse. A lot worse. What's worse than a Creaker . . . ?

You'll see . . .

Chapter Six
THE DAY AFTER

L ucy burst out into the sunlit yard with new-found determination. She didn't want to just dream about her parents for the rest of her life. She wanted them back.

Now.

"That's it," she said to herself. "I'm going to find the grown-ups."

And with that she tightened the straps of her overalls, slicked her bangs over, and marched out into Clutter Avenue.

But something very strange stopped Lucy in her tracks. The disaster movie that Whiffington had looked

74

like the night before wasn't quite as disastrous this morning. The town actually looked relatively tidy!

"That's odd," Lucy said to herself, noticing that all the toilet paper had been cleared from the trees, the overflowing trash cans on the street were now empty, and the pavement looked as though it had been swept clean.

"Where did all the garbage go?" Lucy whispered to herself, searching in her head for any possibilities.

She was so deep in thought that she didn't see it . . .

Lucy gasped as something suddenly tightened about her ankle, like a snake wrapping itself around her leg. Then, before she could do anything about it, she was flipped upside down and yanked straight off the ground, and found herself swinging in the air. She was hanging by her foot from a rope tied to a large tree in someone's front yard.

"GOTCHA!" Norman cried as he sprang out from behind the hedge, his Scout uniform covered in leaves and twigs (he also had a *camouflage* badge, which was so hard to find on his uniform even he'd forgotten where he'd sewn it). When he saw Lucy, his face fell. "Oh, it's you!"

"Yes, it's me! Now get me down!" Lucy demanded.

"Sorry, I thought you were those boys— y'know, the ones from school," Norman said as he cut Lucy free, letting her fall on her head.

"Ouch!" Lucy said. "Boys? What boys?"

"You know, the ones that . . ."

"That what?"

". . . that laugh at me," Norman mumbled.

"Oh," Lucy said, suddenly feeling a little bad for shouting at him.

"They've been throwing eggs at my house since the grown-ups disappeared, so I set some traps for them," Norman said with pride.

Lucy stood up and dusted herself off.

THE DAY AFTER

"Wow!" she said, looking around Norman's front yard, which she now saw he'd turned into a fully functioning campsite. There was a hammock tied between the tree and the drainpipe on Norman's house, and a sundial made of sticks and stones. Scattered along the entire perimeter was an assortment of handmade snares and traps, like the one Lucy had managed to get caught in. There was a campfire with a pan of beans boiling to a bubble on top, and around it some wooden chairs carved from a tree trunk.

"Did you make those?" Lucy asked.

Norman nodded, indicating a *woodwork* badge on his uniform. "And I put that up by myself!" he added, pointing to an enormous green tent pitched on the grass nearby. It was large enough to sleep ten people at least, Lucy thought, although through the opening she could see just one Transformers sleeping bag.

"Why are you sleeping out here, though, and not in your bedroom?" Lucy asked.

Norman suddenly looked a little embarrassed.

"I, erm, well, it's silly really," he said, staring at his feet.

"What is?" Lucy asked.

"Oh, it's nothing . . . I just had a funny dream and got a bit . . ."

"Frightened?" Lucy asked, but Norman was saved from having to answer by the voice that came crashing down the street toward them.

THE DAY AFTER

"Look, it's Abnormal Norman!" called a scruffy kid as he and two more boys on bikes whizzed past.

"AbNorman's got a girlfriend! Hey, love-nerds, eat this!" one of them yelled as the three boys hurled eggs at Norman and Lucy.

"Quick, hold this!" Norman ordered, shoving a metal shield into Lucy's hands. She instinctively held it up in front of her head, feeling the thud, thud, splat of eggs cracking on impact.

"See you loser lovers later," the bike boys cackled as they wheeled off into the distance.

"Are you OK?" Lucy said, lowering the egg-covered shield.

"Me? Yeah, I'm used to it," Norman said, shrugging off the moment. But Lucy could tell by the little twitch of his lip that he was upset.

Lucy had never really taken the time to get to know Norman at school. Of course, she knew who he was. Everyone did. He was "the geeky kid," the one who no one wanted to sit next to at lunch or get paired with in PE. The one who brought a packed lunch instead of eating school lunches, and the one who climbed to the top of the tallest tree and stayed there all the way through break, watching birds through his binoculars. He was . . . different.

Lucy suddenly remembered what her dad would say.

"You know, it's the different people who make a difference," she told him.

Norman blushed. "Yeah, and they get free breakfast!" he replied.

"Huh?"

THE DAY AFTER

"Eggs!" Norman smiled, taking the shield away from Lucy and showing her that it was actually a large frying pan. She laughed as Norman held it over the campfire and began to fry the eggs.

"You can help yourself to some orange squash and a biscuit while you wait . . . if you sign up," Norman said, motioning toward a clipboard he'd attached to his front gate.

"Sign up?" Lucy asked.

"Yes. A crisis is the perfect opportunity to recruit new members for the Whiffington Scout Troop. Girls can join too, you know," Norman said, flipping the eggs.

"Oh, I see. Well, maybe not today . . . ," Lucy said politely. She didn't want to offend him, but joining the Scouts was the last thing on her mind.

"Well, I can't guarantee there'll be a space for you if you don't put your name down today," Norman warned.

"Oh, how many new members have you got?" asked Lucy.

"Well, it's . . . it's still just me, just one member, at the moment. But if my intuition is anything to go by, I'd say interest in the Scout troop is about to pick up in a major way. I've printed flyers and everything. I've got the *intuition* badge, you know," Norman said, proudly showing off a yellow badge with a strange eye on it.

"I see," said Lucy. "And what does your intuition say about finding our parents?"

Norman paused and looked sad.

"I don't know. I mean, that letter sounded pretty final to me."

"I don't believe it for one second," said Lucy. "My mom wouldn't just leave me like that. There's something fishy going on, and I'm going to find out what it is."

"The only fishy thing going on is the smell from your dad's truck. I don't think they're ever coming back, Lucy. Whiffington is *our* town now," Norman said gloomily.

"It's like a nightmare!" Lucy sighed.

Norman's face suddenly scrunched up like he'd smelled a bad smell (and not just the stink coming from Lucy's dad's truck).

The Day After

"What is it?" Lucy asked.

"You just reminded me. I had a nightmare last night," said Norman.

Lucy's heart stopped for a moment.

"So did I," she said.

"Mine was really weird."

"Mine too!"

"I dreamed I saw this *thing* . . ."

"Yes?" Lucy said.

"These shiny, gleaming eyes . . . And it was all dark and shadowy. And it was hiding—"

"UNDER YOUR BED!" Lucy interrupted him. "That's why you came and set the tent up out here, isn't it?"

Norman stared at her. "How did you know that?" he asked.

Lucy looked up at the window of Norman's bedroom. How was it possible for them both to have the same dream? The same nightmare?

Unless it wasn't a nightmare at all.

Unless what they'd both seen in the night, those black eyes, were *real*.

Lucy and Norman stared at one another in silence.

"BOO!" shrieked a high, shrill voice from behind Norman's fence.

"Ella!" Lucy cried, her heart pounding as Ella Noying skipped out into the street wearing an old wedding dress that trailed along behind her.

"I couldn't help it!" Ella laughed. "Your faces!"

"Ella, what are you wearing?" Lucy said in utter disbelief.

"What, *this* old thing? Oh, it used to belong to Mama. I've had it for years, darling." Ella beamed, dragging the dress along the ground as she swished it.

"And what on earth is around your neck?" Norman asked.

"My jewels? They belonged to my dad, but they look far better on me, don't you think?" Ella said, trying to swing the chunky gold chain, which was obviously too heavy for her.

"That's your dad's?" Norman asked.

"Her dad is the mayor of Whiffington. It's part of his uniform," Lucy explained.

"Which means now that he's gone, I am the new

mayor of Whiffington!" Ella announced, completing her look by perching a triangular hat that she'd folded out of paper on top of her bouncy hair. The word *MAYOR* was scribbled in felt-tip pen on the front.

"I'm not sure that's how it works," Norman told her.

"It doesn't matter anyway, because your parents are definitely coming back. Just like my mom is definitely coming back—and Norman's dad too," said Lucy firmly. "So, if I were you, I'd take those things off right now."

Ella ignored Lucy. "Mama isn't here! Mama isn't

here! No one can stop me! Mama isn't here!" she sang merrily as she twirled around like a princess.

Lucy suddenly had a thought.

"Hey, Ella," she said. "What did you dream about last night?"

Ella pretended to think. "Erm . . . can't remember!" she said as she came skipping back down the road toward them.

"Please try! When you woke up this morning, did you remember what you dreamed?"

Ella looked up at Lucy and pretended to zip her lips.

"If you tell us, I'll let you have some eggs!" Norman said, waving the pan temptingly.

Ella's eyes narrowed. "Runny ones?" she asked.

Norman nodded and Ella unzipped her lips at once.

"Well, it was just the same dream I have every night," she said.

"And what's that?" said Lucy.

"It's a funny dream, really," Ella said. "You know, that one when you dream about the creature that lives under your bed."

Lucy and Norman looked at each other.

THE DAY AFTER

"What the jiggins?" Lucy breathed softly.

It was at that moment that Lucy and Norman both realized their nightmare wasn't a nightmare at all. There *had* been something under their beds last night— and Lucy had a funny feeling that this was all connected somehow.

The grown-ups disappearing.

The creatures under the bed.

What could possibly happen next?

Remember when I said, "What's worse than a Creaker?"

CHAPTER SEVEN
FOUR CREAKERS

Lucy jumped into bed that night faster than she'd ever done before. She was so fearful that something might grab her ankles from underneath the bed as she climbed up that she literally leapt from the floorboards to the mattress and pulled her bedcovers up and over her head. She didn't even bother to take off her overalls, brush her teeth, or tidy the house! She left it all messy and grubby.

And what a grubby mess it was!

There were all sorts of trash and litter scattered here, there, and everywhere from the piles of children who had been in and out of her house over the last couple of days. So many crumbs of breakfast cereal had been trodden into the carpet that it felt more like walking on sand. She'd been so busy confiscating dangerous items from silly-billy children today that, unlike yesterday, she hadn't washed the dishes, emptied the trash cans, or done any washing whatsoever.

The house was, quite simply, Dis-Gus-Ting.

But Lucy didn't care about that right now. Her breathing was heavy, and the warmth of her breath soon filled up the small space under her duvet, making it hot and sticky. She tried to be as still and as quiet as she could, listening for any strange sounds, any sign of that creature with those black eyes. But she was so scared and nervous that all she could hear was the sound of her own blood pumping around her body, beating in her eardrums like a persistent drummer who won't shut up when you're trying to think.

As the night wore on and the children of Whiffington grew sleepy from the second day of grown-up-less chaos, the noises from out in the streets began to settle. Soon everything was still. Everything was calm.

That is always when the weirdest things happen.

THE CREAKERS

Lucy heard it.

Her heart stopped.

She recognized it instantly.

She'd walked across her bedroom thousands and thousands of times, and she knew that sound better than anyone: the unmistakable creak of the old wooden floorboards right next to her bed. The floorboards that only ever creaked when someone . . . or some*thing* . . . stepped on them.

Then she heard it again.

Then again.

. . . and once more.

Four times in total.

Then the smell came.

Four Creakers

It was foul and rotten, like a freshly pooped diaper, or spoiled milk. It was so strong that Lucy could hardly even breathe. The thick duvet felt heavy as she hid beneath it, part of her wanting to stay covered, the other desperate to peek out and see what was creaking around her bedroom.

Then she heard something even more terrifying than a creak. She heard sniffing, followed by a delighted . . .

"Ahhhhhhhhh . . ."

It spoke!

Or at least it made a noise.

"This be the place!"

Yep, it definitely spoke. Although it didn't sound like you or me when we speak. This voice was croaky, creaky, disgusting.

"This be where *it* lives . . . ," croaked the creature.

"Shhhhhh, the kidderling be hearin' you. It be hidin' just under the bedcovers," squeaked another one.

"Shall we snatch it up?" scratched a different one, with a voice like nails running down a chalkboard. That was three separate creatures Lucy had counted.

THREE!

The Creakers

There was a silence.

Snatch me up? Lucy thought. *Please don't snatch me up. Don't snatch me up. Don't snatch me up . . .*

"No . . . not this dark," grunted a fourth voice. "Let's just take what we be creakin' for and be gone back to the Woleb."

The Woleb? thought Lucy. *Where on earth is the Woleb?* She'd certainly never heard of anywhere with a name like that.

Suddenly Lucy heard another creak—and then another, and another. These creaks were the sound of someone—or some*thing*—creeping across her bedroom, across the floorboards close to her wardrobe.

They were followed by the sound of her wardrobe door opening.

"Well, where be it?" grunted the grunter.

"It be in 'ere somewhere! I saw the kidderling get it out last dark!" muttered the scratchy one.

They all started rummaging around. Lucy heard hangers clanging and drawers being opened and closed. These creatures weren't trying to be quiet, not tonight.

"It's good fun, innit, not 'avin' to creak around so

quiet neemore, not since we snatched all 'em grown-ups," blabbed the croaky one.

"Shut up, you dunglicker! We be Creakers—we still gotter creak!" huffed the grunter.

Creakers, Lucy thought. *So that's what they're called.* The word made her shudder and her skin crawl with creepiness.

"*It* might be earwiggin'!" added the grunter, and somehow Lucy felt these *Creakers* all looking in her direction on the other side of the duvet.

"So whats if it is. I don't care neemore," screeched the scratcher.

"Let's get that stinkerful green coat and be off," whispered the squeaker.

Lucy suddenly realized what the Creakers were looking for.

My dad's jacket! she thought.

Then she froze as she remembered what was in the jacket pocket: her father's silver harmonica. Her heart began pumping faster and faster. *They can't take my dad's things. They're all I have to remember him by!*

There was a frustrated rattle of hangers from the

wardrobe. "It not be in 'ere!" grumbled the scratchy one.

"That sneaksy little kidder must've hid it somewhere else," croaked the creaky one.

"Check the rest of the house!" ordered the hisser, and Lucy heard the four creatures all move at once, creaking across her wooden floor, out of her bedroom, and into her mom's room across the landing.

I have to stop them from taking Dad's jacket! thought Lucy.

Wait just a creak, Lucy. There are four Creakers creaking around in the next room. You're all alone, hiding beneath your bedcovers. Are you sure you want to try to stop them?

Yes! thought Lucy.

Wow—you're braver than I am, Lucy! OK, good luck!

Lucy gulped as she pulled the corner of her duvet down with trembling hands. She peeked out and saw that her bedroom was empty, but she could hear the creaks and croaks of the creatures searching her mom's room.

"Check them drawers! We wants that coat!" one of the creatures hissed.

Lucy looked at her open wardrobe and at the wooden panel that was still in place, hiding her dad's stinky work coat. Whether it was a moment of courage or pure insanity, Lucy leapt out of bed and legged it straight to her wardrobe. She heaped all her clothes on top of the panel to make sure it stayed well hidden.

"Wait!" hissed a voice, and everything went quiet.

"I smell stink."

"I smell dread!"

"I smell a kidderling outta bed . . . ," croaked the four creatures, and then Lucy heard the most terrifying sound she'd heard all night.

The creatures all started creaking back toward her bedroom.

Lucy's eyes darted around her room. She knew hiding underneath her duvet wasn't going to get her out of this. She couldn't run out of the door, or the Creakers would snatch her. She looked at her bedroom window, but it was far too high to jump from.

Would you be quiet while I'm thinking! Lucy thought.

Who, me? Sorry!

Where can I go? she thought. *Not out of the door, not out of the window. They'll find me in the wardrobe . . . There must be another way.*

That's when she saw it—the shadowy gap beneath her bed.

If these Creakers got into my room that way, then maybe I can get out that way!

The creaks grew louder as the creatures shuffled out of her mom's bedroom and into the hallway just outside her door.

"Gonna snatch that kidderling!" they croaked.

"Gotter finds that grubby coat!" they cried.

Lucy had no time to think it through. It was under the bed, or be snatched by these four things that were about to come creaking through her bedroom door any second!

She bolted toward her bed as fast as her legs could bolt, and just as she got to it she dropped down and slid straight underneath.

For a few moments Lucy lay trembling in the darkness underneath her bed. All of a sudden she began to experience the strangest sensation. The hard wooden floorboards beneath her didn't feel as hard as normal.

In fact, the floor under Lucy's bed didn't feel normal at all.

Four Creakers

Lucy pressed the palms of her hands against it. It was soft and squishy, like bubblegum or warm cookie dough—and before Lucy knew what was happening, she found herself sinking into the floor like quicksand.

She was being pulled into the world below.

She clawed at the floor as it began to swallow her up, but it was no good—she was going into it, whether she liked it or not. The doughy floor tightened as she sank up to her chest, then to her neck, her mouth, her nose, and just as the room above disappeared completely, Lucy caught a glimpse of four pairs of twinkling black eyes peering at her from the doorway.

"The kidderling be goin' down to the Woleb!" they hissed.

And with that Lucy was gone.

Chapter Eight
THE WOLEB

L ucy was sinking, deeper and deeper. Every now and then the floor beneath her bed would stop swallowing her, and the dark, spongy walls around her would loosen and tighten before pulling her down again. She imagined that this was what it must feel like to be eaten whole by a giant snake.

Wherever Lucy was going, whatever this Woleb place was, it felt like she was being sucked through some sort of wormhole, traveling not only down below her bed but also across time and space itself. She began to feel a little queasy, like the time she'd been in training for the family jelly bean–eating competition and she'd puked on her shoes.

She couldn't quite put her finger on why or how, but everything she knew to be real and safe was suddenly uncertain. Up was down, left was right, this way was that. Her mind was spinning with dizziness, and not in a good way, like when you spin around and around in the park and fall over laughing. It was more like that dizziness you get when you ride a roller coaster too many times and feel like your head is stuck to the ground and you can't stand up.

Lucy's arms soon started feeling wobbly and tired. Her legs felt like they were made of mashed potato, and she realized she was losing her fight with the floor. But oddly enough, the very second Lucy stopped struggling and wriggling, the walls seemed to let her go.

Her feet came out first as she plopped out of a hole and fell a few yards, but before she landed she stopped in midair, just hovering like one of those astronauts on the International Space Station.

Yep, Lucy was floating, just above the ground. Except the ground wasn't beneath her feet now—it was above her head, and everything was the wrong way up! The moment Lucy realized this she went toppling up to it with a wet thud, landing next to the hole she'd plopped out of.

Lucy was in the Woleb.

"Whatever the Woleb is," she muttered.

She stood up (which was now down) and brushed herself off (which was now on), and her head began to feel all twisted with this backwardness. She took a step forward (which was now backward) and stumbled a little as the ground wobbled under her bare feet. It was the strangest thing she'd ever stepped on. It felt warm, damp, and squelchy, like standing on a giant tongue.

Yuck! thought Lucy. *I wish I'd worn my slippers!*

That's the thing about having adventures in the middle of the night. You can never be fully prepared for them.

The air was hot and misty down here in this soggy corridor, and

Lucy felt her T-shirt begin to stick to her arms and back. She slicked her bangs out of her eyes and they stayed there, stuck in place on the side of her forehead by small drops of sweat.

The walls were slightly rounded, with ridges on them that arched up over Lucy's head as though she were standing in a giant throat. The thought made her shiver. It also stank—it was so disgustingly rotten that Lucy could feel her eyes watering, and she had to hold her nose.

Suddenly the hole by her feet started wobbling like mud-flavored jelly, and Lucy noticed a small wooden signpost next to it with one word written on it: *Dungston.* Her surname—and Lucy recognized the writing instantly. It was the same sticky brown writing that had been used in the letter she'd found pinned to the school door.

"So the Creakers wrote that letter!" she muttered to herself as she studied the messy handwriting.

The hole wobbled again, and a moment later she heard voices echoing through it. Voices, and laughter, and cackling.

103

The Creakers.

"They must be following me down!" she gasped.

Lucy had no choice but to keep moving deeper into the Woleb, or they would catch up with her and snatch her. She started running as best she could, but it was like being on a bouncy castle, or in those dreams when you're running and not getting anywhere. Lucy puffed and panted, and her chest felt tight as she struggled for breath. *I've got to slow down,* she realized.

Then, just like the backwardness of the upside-down floor, as Lucy slowed down and began walking, everything suddenly felt easier, and she realized she could move faster.

She only managed to sprint a few slow steps before her foot hit something, tripping her up. She bounced on the wobbly, wet ground with a disgusting squelch, and as she came to a halt, out of the corner of her eye Lucy caught sight of the thing that had tripped her.

It was another small wooden signpost in the squishy floor, just like the one she'd seen with her surname on it.

When Lucy read what this sign said, her heart leapt with hope.

It said *Quirk* in exactly the same sloppy brown writing. And next to the signpost she saw a small hole, just like the one that she'd plopped out of.

Norman Quirk! That has to be Norman's house through there! Lucy thought as she peered into the small opening. She could just make out a dark bedroom at the other end of it.

Lucy looked around and saw another signpost just a few feet away. Then another, and another: there were hundreds, maybe thousands of these little wooden signposts dotted all around her, stretching into the distance of the Woleb, poking out of the steamy mist like tombstones in a graveyard.

She began to read all the names scrawled on them. *Noying, Badding, Payne, Green, Trundle, Cobblesmith . . .*

It's Clutter Avenue! Lucy realized.

As she stared at the positions of these signs, Lucy could tell that they all matched perfectly with the houses and streets and buildings of Whiffington Town. Next to each post was its own small round opening, like a portal, joining this backward place with the world above.

"Oh, little kidderling!" a menacing grunt echoed off the wet walls. "You's not s'posed to be down in the Woleb."

Lucy spun around. Through the mist she saw four pairs of small, black, beady eyes staring at her.

Her heart froze midbeat. She could barely make out these four creatures through the haze, but their piercing eyes were enough to make her want to get as far away from them as possible. Quickly she looked around at the long, wet, twisted route of the Woleb, which seemed to go on and on, deeper into the ground.

I don't really want to go down there! she thought.

Good idea, Lucy! (Although what Lucy didn't know was that in a few chapters she would be going much deeper into the Woleb.)

What? thought Lucy.

OH, NOTHING! Carry on—you were about to escape!

Oh, right! thought Lucy.

She took a deep breath, slicked her bangs over, and dived headfirst into the jellylike hole next to Norman Quirk's signpost, hoping, wishing, praying that it led to her world!

"She's crawlin' backs up!" one of the Creakers hissed from somewhere behind her.

"Too late to get 'er now," grumbled another.

"We'll have to snatch 'er tomorrow . . . ," another one creaked—and then the wobbly walls grabbed her and sucked her in deeper, and Lucy could no longer hear them.

THE CREAKERS

The sensation of going back down (or was it up?) the tight, squishy wormhole was just as weird as when it had swallowed her the first time. Lucy closed her eyes tight and held her breath as the walls wriggled and twisted like they were alive, pushing her along until they spat her into the darkness underneath another bed.

She opened her eyes. Her heart was pounding, and her breath came in shaky gasps.

She was back in Whiffington, in someone else's bedroom.

"Hello?" she whispered, but there was no reply.

She crawled out from under the bed, and her legs wobbled as she stood up in the small room, still feeling the effects of the backward Woleb. The room was covered with all sorts of bits and pieces, from maps and camping stoves to fishing rods and rope ladders and the biggest collection of Transformers toys Lucy had ever seen. There was also an iron and ironing board with a neatly pressed, badge-covered uniform ready for the morning, and hanging on the wall was a photo of a young boy and his father, both in full Scout uniforms, holding a huge fish between them and wearing even bigger smiles stretched across their proud faces.

Definitely Norman's house! thought Lucy, and raced for the door.

"Norman?!" she called, running downstairs as fast as she could. She yanked open the front door, and to her surprise she was blinded by sunlight as it engulfed her face with warm kindness.

It was morning!

"Lucy?" Norman said, waking up in his hammock, and shielding his eyes from the sun. "Monsters under the bed again?"

"No . . . *Creakers!*" Lucy replied.

The hammock swung and swayed as Lucy climbed up next to Norman and told him all about it.

Chapter Nine
THE PLAN

"**B**limey!" Norman gawked as Lucy tried to explain about the backwards world beneath their beds. "So you think that's where our parents are, in that Woleb?"

"Yep!" Lucy said. "That's what the Creakers said! They *snatched* them!"

"And they want your dad's jacket?"

"Uh-huh. Although I have no idea why."

"And they're coming back to snatch you tonight?"

Lucy looked at him and nodded.

"Blimey," Norman said again.

"Double blimey!" Lucy added with a worried frown.

Norman rustled up a Scout's breakfast of egg and beans on his camping stove, but by the time they sat down to eat, they were both so full of worry that neither of them had much of an appetite.

"Shall we go for a walk, clear our heads?" Norman suggested, noticing that Lucy hadn't eaten a single baked bean.

Lucy smiled and nodded again. But as they wandered into the street, it soon became clear that Whiffington no longer looked like Whiffington at all. The kids had been alone for approximately forty-nine hours and things had started to get a little . . .

Well, let's take a look at the chaos Lucy and Norman saw.

Billy Noshling had put his head inside the

vending machine and munched all two hundred bags of chips (even the salt-and-vinegar-flavored ones). Unfortunately, he now couldn't get his head back out again. The only way to free him would be to put some money in the machine and buy him, but since there were no grown-ups around to give the children pocket money, he had no choice but to stay there.

Jackson Gilly had released three sharks into the public swimming pool and tried opening a small aquarium. However, he's forgotten to mention the sharks to the children who were using the pool at the time.

One whole street had had its pavement replaced with trampolines, and the rec center had its trampolines replaced with pavement. Neither arrangement worked out very well.

Four children had accidentally flushed themselves down the toilet, clogging the pipes for the rest of the town.

And, worst of all, Scrummy McScroodles Sweets 'n' Stuff had run out of sweets and now only had stuff.

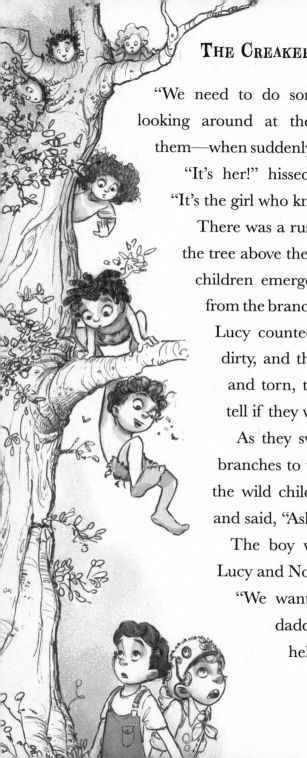

THE CREAKERS

"We need to do something!" Lucy said, looking around at the chaos surrounding them—when suddenly they heard a whisper.

"It's her!" hissed the voice excitedly. "It's the girl who knows what to do!"

There was a rustle, and the leaves on the tree above them parted. A group of children emerged, clambering down from the branches like wild monkeys. Lucy counted six of them, all so dirty, and their clothes so ragged and torn, that it was difficult to tell if they were boys or girls.

As they swung down from the branches to the pavement, one of the wild children nudged another and said, "Ask her! Go on!"

The boy was shoved closer to Lucy and Norman.

"We want our mommies and daddies back. P-p-please help us," the filthy child said, his wild eyes suddenly large and worried, so that he looked like a sad kitten.

"Food . . . ," another one whispered while crouching beside the tree.

"And food," added the first child. "Do you have any food?"

Lucy looked at Norman. Things had turned from bad to worse. It wasn't fun anymore. The novelty of having no grown-ups around was wearing off fast. These kids were tired and hungry.

"I've got some eggs and beans you can have," offered Norman. "They're still in the pan in my —"

Before Norman could finish his sentence, the wild children scurried down the street in the direction Norman and Lucy had come from, in search of his food.

"OK, you're right. We need to do something!" Norman admitted. "But *what*?"

"I need to go to the Woleb and get the grown-ups back," Lucy said, staring after the wild kids.

"I was afraid you were going to say that," said Norman, wiping the sweat from his forehead with his yellow Scout scarf. "But how are you going to do it? You don't know your way around the Woleb. You've got no idea how big it is or where it leads or whereabouts they're keeping our parents. It's impossible." He sighed. "Unless . . ."

"Unless what?" Lucy asked hopefully.

"Unless we somehow manage to get one of those Creakers to take us to the grown-ups." Norman gazed into the distance, deep in thought.

Lucy grabbed his arm. "Norman. That's a brilliant idea! But—how are we going to do it?"

"Whatcha doin'?" squeaked Ella Noying, popping out suddenly from behind them, making them both jump.

"ELLA!" Norman gasped.

Lucy cried, "Have you been following us?"

"Maybe," said Ella.

Norman and Lucy looked at each other.

"How much did you hear?" Lucy asked.

"Only ALL OF IT!" sang Ella in an awful, over-the-top operatic voice, flinging her arms around like a diva. "I heard it all! I heard it AAALL! **AAALL!**" she wailed in a painful, screeching voice.

THE PLAN

"Ella, you can't tell anyone what you heard!" Lucy shouted, cupping her hand over Ella's mouth to shut her up. "It's a secret. Er, yuck! She licked my hand!" she cried, snatching it away from Ella's grinning mouth.

"Puh-lease, I'm six years old," Ella said with a dismissive wave of her hand. "I know there's no such thing as monsters under the bed. Your silly stories don't scare me, you know."

"*Stories* . . . right," said Norman with a naughty little twinkle in his eye. "Hey, Ella, if you're so brave, why don't you come to our ghost-story sleepover tonight at Lucy's house?"

"What?!" cried Lucy.

Norman quickly shot her a look that said, *Play along*.

"Right! Yeah, I forgot! A sleepover . . . ," Lucy said as she realized what Norman was up to. She bit her lip to hide a smile. Norman really wasn't so bad after all.

"It'll be fun! We'll stay up past midnight and everything," Norman added.

"Midnight? Really! Come on, Norm. That's, like, *sooooo* early. Millie Butkins was awake until one a.m. last night. You gotta do better than that."

"OK, fine. One a.m!" Norman agreed. "Are you in?"

Ella looked suspiciously at them both for a moment before shrugging her shoulders. "If you throw in a full bag of marshmallows, then you can count me in."

"Deal!" Norman said, and they shook hands.

Ella skipped merrily off toward Trampoline Avenue, leaving Norman and Lucy alone.

"Two words," Norman said as they watched Ella disappearing into the distance. "Live bait."

Almond milk
Butter
Eggs
Toilet paper
Toothpaste
AA batteries
Dark chocolate

*Oh, sorry! I needed somewhere to write my shopping list.
Back to the story . . .*

Chapter Ten
THE CREAKER TRAP

The plan was simple. Lucy needed to get down into the Woleb and find the grown-ups—and, to do that, she needed to catch a Creaker. It was going to be a bit like fishing, Norman had explained to her, which was one of his favorite things to do with his dad—and Ella Noying was the bait.

Not just Ella, in fact—but Ella wearing Lucy's dad's stinking work coat.

"It's perfect!" said Norman. "We'll make Ella wear your dad's smelly jacket, and the Creakers will sniff it out, see a little girl wearing it in the middle of your bedroom, think that Ella is you, and then try to snatch you—and when they do, that's when we'll trap them!"

THE CREAKER TRAP

Now, it's not very nice to use little girls as live bait to catch monsters, but if you ever have to, then it's always best to use an annoying little sprog like Ella, just in case they do actually end up getting snatched. That way at least you won't have to put up with them anymore.

"Don't worry!" Norman added quickly, seeing that Lucy was looking uncertain about this plan. "I'm about eighty-seven percent confident that we'll catch a Creaker before it gets anywhere near Ella."

Norman and Lucy agreed that this was an acceptable risk in such extreme circumstances, and so they went straight back to Lucy's house to lay Creaker traps. But, to Lucy's surprise, her house wasn't quite as she had left it.

"It's . . . clean?!" she said as she looked around at the mess-free house. The night before, she'd been too scared to tidy up. She'd just leapt into bed, leaving the house in a sloppy state. But today it was spotless.

"How odd!" Lucy said. "The house was a complete pigsty yesterday. There was trash everywhere! *I* didn't clean it up, and no one else has been in here except . . ."

She paused for a moment, and her eyes opened wide.

"The Creakers!" they both shouted at the same time.

Norman shook his head. "Wait a minute. Are you saying that the monsters under your bed, the ones that snatched away all the grown-ups and live in that creepy world beneath us, decided to have a quick spring cleaning before chasing you down that hole last night?"

"Looks like it!" Lucy said, shrugging.

"I wonder why . . . ," Norman pondered, scratching his neatly combed hair thoughtfully.

"What are you thinking?" asked Lucy, intrigued by Norman's pensive silence.

"Well, any half-decent Scout knows that the best way to catch something is to work out what it wants. The Creakers are coming back for your dad's disgusting coat, right?"

"Yeah . . ."

"You said you left the house like a complete dump?"

"Yep . . ."

"And when you came back, all the mess was gone?"

"Right!"

"So, maybe . . ." Norman thought for a moment. "Maybe that tells us something about these Creakers. Maybe they love **TRASH!**"

"What?!" said Lucy, finding that idea a little weird.

"Think about it! You said yourself that the Woleb was all disgusting and stinky. Well, maybe they take all our dirty, mucky stuff down there," Norman said.

Lucy opened her mouth to argue but found that nothing came out. Sometimes that's how you realize that someone else is right.

"Let's make a Creaker trap!" Norman grinned.

They spent the rest of the afternoon cobbling together the craftiest Creaker trap they could think of. Lucy was pretty good at it, but Norman, with his scouting expertise, was amazing!

He rolled out a large sheet of paper and drew a map of Lucy's room.

"This is only rough. If I'd had more time, I would have drawn a more accurate plan," Norman said apologetically.

"Norman, it looks amazing!" said Lucy, staring at the incredibly detailed drawing spread out in front of her, on which Norman had written **NORMAN + LUCY'S CREAKER TRAP PLAN!** in big letters.

Here's a copy of the plan:

Together, they set to work collecting the most horrid, stinking leftovers from the back of Lucy's dad's garbage truck. Norman showed Lucy how to lay out a trail of the rotten stuff leading from the shadows of her bed to the center of the room. At the end of the trail, they marked an **E** with a piece of chalk. That would be Ella's spot. Next to it, Norman wrote a **C** for *Creaker*, over which they hung Lucy's mom's extra-large laundry basket.

"That'll drop down and catch 'em!" Norman explained as he rigged the basket to a complicated pulley system of skipping ropes, which wound around the room and finished inside Lucy's wardrobe. "That's where you'll hide, ready to release the basket," he added.

"Where will you be?" Lucy asked.

"I'll wait on the bed, ready to jump on the basket once it lands on them," Norman said, sounding surprisingly brave. "What are we going to do once we've got them?"

"I'm going to make Ella sing to them until they tell me where they're keeping the grown-ups," Lucy said, and they both laughed as they admired their masterpiece.

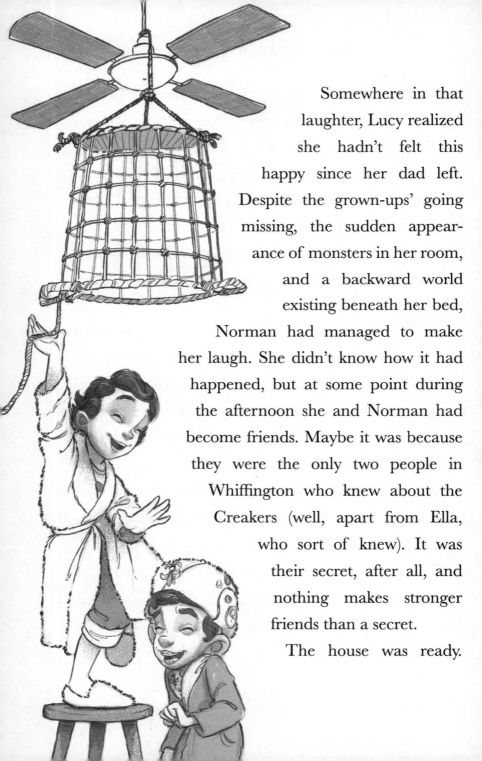

Somewhere in that laughter, Lucy realized she hadn't felt this happy since her dad left. Despite the grown-ups' going missing, the sudden appearance of monsters in her room, and a backward world existing beneath her bed, Norman had managed to make her laugh. She didn't know how it had happened, but at some point during the afternoon she and Norman had become friends. Maybe it was because they were the only two people in Whiffington who knew about the Creakers (well, apart from Ella, who sort of knew). It was their secret, after all, and nothing makes stronger friends than a secret.

The house was ready.

The trap was set. Now they just needed to wait for the Creakers to return . . .

"Why do I have to wear this rotten thing?" Ella whined as they sat her down in the middle of Lucy's room, right on the **E** marked on the floor.

"Oh, it just makes the ghost stories scarier. You know, the bad smell and all that . . . ," Norman lied.

"Yeah, erm . . . it adds to the effect!" Lucy added.

"OK," said Ella uncertainly as the massive stinking coat swamped her shoulders, covering up her silky pink pajamas. Norman and Lucy both had their bathrobes on to hide their clothes underneath. Norman was wearing his full Scout uniform, and Lucy was in her favorite pair of overalls, so although they looked ready for a sleepover, they were fully prepared for adventure.

"Why is your room so messy?" asked Ella, looking around.

"Because Mom's not here to tidy it up!" lied Lucy, feeling the butterflies fluttering in her tummy. She hated lying, even to Ella Noying.

"So where are they?" Ella said, holding out her hands expectantly.

"Here you go. A full bag of marshmallows, as requested," Lucy said, plonking it into Ella's open hands.

"Oooooh, goodie-goodie, nom-nom!" said Ella, ripping open the bag at once and beginning to munch on the sweets, picking out all her favorite pink ones.

They switched off Lucy's bedroom light, huddled around Norman's flashlight, and spent the rest of the night sharing spooky stories like "The Haunted Treehouse," "Night of the Living Dead Goldfish," and Norman's personal favorite, "The Campsite Critters of Cold Creek."

"Those stories weren't scary at all!" Ella whined. "You two are terrible! I thought we were going to tell *really* scary ones. You two are big scaredy-cats!"

All of a sudden a bell chimed from the church on the other side of Whiffington Town, echoing through the darkness of the night outside Lucy's window.

"Oh, listen to that! It's midnight," Ella said, looking a little excited.

"That's right, Ella, and do you know what happens at midnight?" asked Lucy.

"Norman's head turns back into a pumpkin?" Ella giggled.

"No. It's when the Creakers come out . . . ," Lucy said.

Ella fell silent and stopped chewing her mouthful of pink marshmallows.

"The *what*?"

"Creakers. You *have* heard of the Creakers, haven't you?" Norman said.

"Yeah . . . oh, Creakers, of course! Sure, I know all about Creakers. I probably know more than both of you, actually," Ella replied. Lucy could tell she was fibbing. "But maybe you could just remind me . . ."

"Creakers are the things that hide under your bed," said Lucy.

"Creakers are the things that put nasty dreams inside your head," added Norman.

"I'm not scared of those silly things. It's just a story," lied Ella.

"That's what most children think, Ella, but there's only one way to be sure a Creaker doesn't get you in the night," Norman said, making his voice as spooky as he could (which wasn't very).

"What's that?" asked Ella.

"To stay up *all* night," Norman said.

"And not go to bed," added Lucy.

Ella started to look a little uneasy, like she wanted to go back to telling the not-so-scary stories.

"Right, I'm off to sleep!" said Norman chirpily, switching off his flashlight and climbing into Lucy's bed. "Nighty night!"

"Wait, you're actually going to bed? What if a Creaker comes?!" whined Ella.

"It's just a story, like you said!" Norman yawned, rolling over and pulling the covers over his head.

"You know, I'm feeling sleepy too!" said Lucy, climbing into the wardrobe, which she'd lined with a duvet and pillow. She closed the door until she could just see Ella through a small crack.

"Are you both bonkers?" Ella cried. "If these Creaky things creak out and you're both fast asleep, you'll both be goners! We've got to stay up all night!" She huddled on the floor, keeping a careful eye on the shadows underneath the bed.

Right on the spot marked with an **E**.

"OK, we'll take turns. You take the first watch, Ella," Lucy said, smiling to herself as she settled into her little nest inside the wardrobe. Even though she couldn't see him, she knew that Norman was smiling too. Their plan was working.

For now . . .

CHAPTER ELEVEN

CATCHING CREAKERS

L ucy and Norman lay very still, silently pretending to sleep as they listened for the first signs of a Creaker. Ella remained sitting on her spot on the floor, too scared to move and too scared to sleep. She just sat there, wishing for the sun to come up and for this scary, spooky night to be over.

The perfect Creaker bait.

There was no way Lucy was going to fall asleep tonight, not with the risk of losing her dad's jacket to a bunch of creepy creatures from under her bed. As she stared at the inside of her wardrobe and her eyes adjusted to the dark, she began to see the things inside.

Her second- and third-favorite pairs of overalls hanging overhead; her shoes piled in the corner. And then something else caught her eye. Some writing on the inside of the door. It was a chart, measuring her height over the years. Of course, it was right there every time she opened her wardrobe, but it was one of those things she'd seen so often that it had become invisible to her.

Now that she had time to really look at it, she realized how amazing it was to see how small she'd once been, and how much she'd grown. But as she studied it in the thin crack of light coming in through the slightly open door, she realized what was so special about it. Scribbled with a marker pen next to the chart was the word *Lucy*, and Lucy recognized her dad's handwriting: the distinctive way he wrote his *Y*s, with the extra loop in the tail. Her heart fluttered a little at seeing this piece of her dad that she'd forgotten was there.

She couldn't remember when the chart had started. She squinted in the dim light and looked at the very lowest marking on the chart, close to her feet. The words *AGE 2 AND 7 MONTHS* were written there, in her mom's neat handwriting.

133

As her name moved higher and higher up the door and the ages next to it grew older, Lucy spotted something right near the top.

There was some more writing way up high. Far too high to be Lucy's height. Carefully and quietly she stood up in the wardrobe to get a better look. As she got closer, she read the words *MOM—AGE 32,* and a little farther up was *Dad—Age 34*.

Lucy had a sudden, unexpected feeling. Her whole body felt warm and safe, like she was being hugged. Just seeing the words *MOM* and *Dad* written in her parents' handwriting brought back those feelings that only families can give to each other. She felt comforted for a moment, snug in the wardrobe, as though somehow the grown-up-less world outside didn't exist. Like her family was back together again, the three of them, right there in the wardrobe.

Her happy moment was interrupted by the chiming of the clock tower echoing across Whiffington, announcing the hour.

It must be getting late, thought Lucy as she counted the chimes.

Catching Creakers

Three in the morning already? she thought. *That went fast!*

And that's when she heard it.

Not a creak but a yawn. It was Ella.

Lucy peered out of the crack in the wardrobe door and saw Ella stretching sleepily before rubbing her tired eyes. *Obviously our scary Creaker story wasn't scary enough to keep Ella awake all night,* she thought.

Then Lucy heard something else.

Another yawn.

This time it was Norman.

That useless boy! Lucy thought, watching him snuggle comfortably in her bed and start snoozing on her pillow.

But Lucy had the feeling that something wasn't quite right. She peeped out of her hiding place in the wardrobe again and saw the most astonishing thing.

A faint cloud of golden dust was wafting across her room, settling over the eyes of Ella and Norman as it floated by.

Lucy's heart stopped. Ella and Norman weren't

falling asleep. They were being *sent* to sleep! She watched the dust settle into the corners of their eyes as they drifted deeper into hypnotic slumber.

Then Lucy realized that Ella's and Norman's sleepy eyes weren't the only eyes she could see.

They were there.

Four pairs of beady black eyeballs were lurking in the shadows beneath her bed, staring out.

Lucy froze inside the wardrobe. But the eyes weren't looking at Lucy. They hadn't seen her yet. They were looking at Ella, wrapped up in the jacket, and at all the deliciously rotten bits of trash scattered temptingly around Lucy's room.

"They be a-good and dozyin' now," croaked a voice from the darkness. "Dozy Dust always be workin' a treat!"

"Them kidderlings not be wakin' up for a long time this night," grunted another. "Stupid girl brung a weedy little boy with her. Ergh, look! It's the tidy kidderling from across the walk. He won't be doin' 'er ne-help." They all laughed.

This is good, thought Lucy. The Creakers thought that

Ella, curled up in the fluorescent jacket, was her. Just as she and Norman had planned.

"Come on. Let's be gettin' the stinkerin' coat," hissed another.

With that, Lucy saw movement in the shadows. Her tummy was full of fluttery wobbles, her mouth dropped open in shock, goose bumps pimpled down both arms, and the hairs on the back of her neck stood up as the four Creakers crept out of the blackness and she caught sight of them for the very first time.

Their skin was dark green and shimmered with a sticky wetness, like the repulsive flesh of a slug. They had veiny ears that looked like rotten cabbage leaves and long, pointy claws that seemed to click across the floor like spiders' legs as they crept. Each of them dragged a rotten tail behind, which looked like a moldy brown banana skin.

One by one, they stood up, revealing their full rottenness. Their heads were just high enough to poke over the side of Lucy's bed.

Lucy squinted in the dimness. From her hiding spot inside the cupboard she could see them clearly . . .

One of them was freckled with boils and pus-filled spots along its gangly arms.

Another's sticky skin had dry flaky patches peeling off, reminding Lucy of the time she'd gotten sunburned on vacation.

The chubbiest one had matted, waxy hair poking out

of its oversized ears and a belly like a small round cannonball.

The last one to emerge from the dark had a layer of spikes on its back like uncut fingernails poking out in every direction.

This one was their leader. Lucy could tell by the way the rest creaked out of his way as he crept along the wooden floorboards and into her room.

The sight of them made Lucy gag. They were the most hideous things she'd ever seen. But their disgustingness was only just beginning.

"Oooh, looky this!" the flabby round one said, holding up a rotten slice of pizza with fluffy green mold oozing from the crust. Norman had salvaged it from the garbage truck earlier, thinking it would be great Creaker bait. *He was right!* thought Lucy, making a face as the Creaker gave it a greedy sniff.

"Puts it down, Guff. We's 'ere for one thing this night," hissed the leader.

Guff? What an awful name, Lucy thought.

Guff let out an awful gassy "burp" from his little fat bottom, and Lucy realized how he had gotten his name.

"But, Grunt, looks at alls the treasures. The room be covered nice 'n' rotten!" said Guff, looking at the trail laid out across the floor.

Grunt? That's an even worse name than Guff! thought Lucy, but Grunt—the one with the prickly nails on his back and a rotten scowl on his face—seemed to suit his name too.

"Guff's right. We gotter take this stinkerin' stuff, Grunt. It be too good to—"

"Waste!" blurted out the one with horrid boils, interrupting the one with flaky skin.

"Don't speaks when I'm speaksin', Sniff, you rotten twizzle!"

"Sorry, Scratch. Sorry. I forgets every time," Sniff said with a nervous chuckle.

"Scratch! Sniff! Be quiet," huffed Grunt.

Grunt, Guff, Scratch, and Sniff. Lucy repeated their names to herself in her head. They were repulsive names for repulsive creatures.

"Fine. If you wants the garbage, we better be creakin' swift and quicky," Grunt said, and with those words the four Creakers began doing the grossest, most peculiar thing. They stretched out their sticky, wet arms and legs and began rolling around the room. As they rolled over the oozing pizza slices, the empty cereal boxes, the old sandwich crusts, the single dirty shoe, the leftovers from dinner, and every disgusting bit of trash, Lucy saw it all

start sticking to their slimy skin. When they finally stopped rolling and stood up, the floor was clean—and the Creakers were covered from sticky head to flaky toe.

It was the strangest thing Lucy had ever witnessed. Four odd little creatures coated in litter and garbage!

Grunt, Guff, Scratch, and Sniff looked at each other and saw how completely covered they were in the mess. Then, one by one, they started laughing.

Now, Creakers don't laugh like you and I do. They come from a backward world where right is wrong, where good is bad, and where laughter sounds more like the wailing of a newborn baby. They howled for nearly five minutes, reveling in the splendid rottenness of their find, and just as Lucy started to wonder if their laughter might wake up Ella and Norman, Sniff reached his oily black claw into a pouch tied around his neck and pulled out a pinch more of their golden dust.

"Justs to be safes . . . ," Sniff said, and he blew the Dozy Dust into the air, where it floated like crumbly magic into the corners of Ella's and Norman's sleepy eyes once again.

"No chances of 'em stoppin' us this time," Sniff added, before snorting like a pig.

Lucy's heart raced. The Creakers didn't know she was hiding in the wardrobe—but if they did, they would surely use their magic sleeping dust on her too.

Then she had an idea. In fact, the idea was dangling right over her head. Her bathing suit was on a hanger— and looped around the top of it were her swimming goggles. She quickly reached up and stretched them over her head, protecting her eyes from any stray crumbs of Dozy Dust.

"Now let's get 'er rotten jacket and be takin' it back to the Woleb," hissed Grunt, creaking toward Ella.

The three other Creakers followed behind him, moving as a shadowy pack into the center of the room, a dark glob of sliminess creeping up on Ella, who was slumped in a slumberous heap. They stretched out their claws, reaching for the grubby jacket, heading right toward the spot on the floor marked with a C.

Right where Lucy wanted them . . .

Chapter Twelve
GRUNT, GUFF, SCRATCH, AND SNIFF

Lucy looked up at the heavy laundry basket dangling from the ceiling, then back down at the four Creakers.

One . . . more . . . step, Lucy thought, *and I've . . .*

GOT YOU!

She released the Creaker trap. The skipping rope unraveled around the hangers and swished out of the wardrobe so fast she could barely see it whiz across the room. In a great crash and clatter, the washing basket came crashing down from above, trapping the Creakers under it and sending the garbage they'd collected flying off in all directions.

"No!" growled Grunt.

"Ouch!" burbled Guff.

"Geroff me!" shrieked Scratch.

"We be trapped!" squealed Sniff.

The Creakers cried out in panic, and Lucy leapt out of the wardrobe, heart ringing like an alarm clock in her chest.

"It's the kidderling!" Grunt croaked. "She were sneakerin' in the wardrobe!"

"What a trickster!" said Guff.

"Yes, a naughty little—"

"Rotter!" Sniff cried, interrupting Scratch, who boshed him on the head. "Sorry!"

Grunt quickly took charge, plunging his black claw into the pouch around Sniff's neck and pulling out a pinch of their golden dust. He puffed it straight at Lucy, and all the Creakers watched eagerly as it swished through the air, straight toward her face, as though the dust itself had a mind of its own and was reaching out with golden, crumbly fingers. But instead of finding her eyes, the Dozy Dust hit the tinted lenses of her swimming goggles and fell uselessly to the floor.

Sniff gasped in horror and fainted in shock. No kidderling—*sorry*—child had ever fended off a Dozy Dust attack before.

"You crafty little sprog!" Grunt spat.

"Did you sees that? The kidder gots freaky Dust Stoppers!" Guff mumbled in a panic.

Scratch kicked Sniff in the belly. "Sniff! Sniff, it's me, Scratch! Wake—"

"Up!" Sniff said, coming around.

"She be a crafty little kidderling, this 'un," Grunt growled, glaring at Lucy.

Suddenly he began clawing at the floor through the woven bars of the upside-down basket, which was barely big enough to hold all four of them. The other Creakers copied him, digging their claws into the wooden floor and scratching away. Slowly the whole laundry basket began to move across the floor toward the bed. It wasn't heavy enough to stop them, and with Norman knocked out with Dozy Dust, there was no one to weigh it down.

Lucy gulped hard, swallowing her fear, and sprinted across the room. She jumped up on top of the laundry basket, pushing it back down again, trapping the Creakers underneath.

"Let us out! Let us out!" the Creakers croaked.

"No, I will not let you out!" Lucy said with a nervous wobble in her voice as she crouched above these monsters. It was terrifying, not being able to see what the Creakers were up to under her feet, but she didn't dare get down in case they made a run for it. As she peeped over the edge, the Creakers were hidden in shadow. Just their long, creepy claws could be seen as they scratched at the floor.

Lucy wished she could turn on the light, but the switch was on the other side of the bedroom. If only she had . . .

NORMAN'S FLASHLIGHT!

She could see it lying on the bed next to him—but could she reach it?

"What's the kidderling doin'?" Guff muttered nervously from below.

"Can't see the rotter!" groaned Grunt.

"She be stretchin' out for somethin'," croaked Scratch.

"She's got a . . . **ARGHHHHH!** The bright!

The bright!" Sniff cried in pain as Lucy flicked on the flashlight and shined it down through the bars of the basket, trying to see these Creakers up close.

"Turns the bright off, you horrid little kidderling! It be too hot!" Grunt cried, cowering away from the flashlight.

Lucy suddenly caught a whiff of something horrid. It smelled like burning hair, all smoky and dry. She realized that the Creakers didn't just dislike the flashlight. It was hurting them. *Burning* them.

"Oh . . . I'm so sorry!" Lucy said, switching off the flashlight right away. These creatures were awfully disgusting, but she didn't want to hurt them. No creature deserved that. Plus, the smell of their burning flesh was horrendous!

"Yes, that's a nice kidderling," gasped Guff, dabbing at his smoldering skin. "Now, just be liftin' up this trapper, and we be on our ways. Leavin' you and your friends alone, yes," he added, peering up at Lucy with his black eyeballs.

"Ella! Norman!" Lucy said, suddenly remembering her friends. Gently she prodded Ella, who was lying next to the basket. "Ella, it's me, Lucy. Can you hear me?"

But Ella didn't open her eyes. She was snoring happily in a blissful snooze.

"Oh, I wouldn't be tryin' to wake up a dozer," said Sniff helpfully. "Nots good to wake someone who's had the dust. Makes 'em all messy in the noggin.'"

"'Messy in the noggin'? 'Had the dust'?" Lucy asked, confused.

"Yes, kidderlings go right out with a bit of Dozy Dust, leavin' it all nice and easy-peasy for us to creak about—Ow!" groaned Sniff as Grunt elbowed him in his round belly.

"Quiet, bog-brain! You be tellin' the human too much," Grunt snapped.

"No! Don't stop!" said Lucy. "That's why I've trapped you. I want answers, and you're not going anywhere until I get them!"

The Creakers went silent, and Lucy sensed them all looking at each other inside the basket beneath her feet.

"We not be tellin' the kidderling a thing," she heard Grunt hiss firmly to the others. More loudly, he added, "We be waitin' for more Creakers to come free us."

"Then you be in a whole heap of the troubles," whispered Scratch threateningly, with a sly smile in his voice.

"What *other* Creakers?" said Guff curiously, rubbing his cannonball tummy. "I didn't know anyone else be comin' 'ere tonight."

"Shut your mud-hole, you mush-minded moron!" Grunt barked.

"Oh, right, sorry! Yeah, them *others* . . . ," Guff quickly said, trying to play along, but Lucy knew now that no one else was coming.

Suddenly she had an idea. There *was* a way she could look at the Creakers—her bedroom mirror! She quickly whipped around to face the wall where her full-length mirror was hanging, positioned perfectly to reflect those wicked creatures underneath.

"There you are." She smiled and put her hands on her hips.

"Ellooo!" waved Sniff chirpily, before being elbowed in the nose by Scratch.

"Now, I want you to tell me exactly what you've done with the grown-ups," Lucy said.

"No," huffed Grunt firmly, staring back out at her in the mirror.

"I want to know why you took them," Lucy calmly explained.

"Nots a chance."

"I want to know why you creak around our bedrooms at night."

"Can't tell the kidder our secrets!"

"And I want you to tell me how I can get the grown-ups back," said Lucy.

"Wah! Wah! Wah!" wailed Grunt, which Lucy remembered was the Creaker way of laughing. "Get the grown-ups back! Wah, wah! That be impossible, you silly kidder."

Lucy's stomach twisted at the word *impossible*.

"I'm not silly. Nothing's impossible," she said. "Impossible isn't real. It's just in your mind! If you tell me where the grown-ups are, I'll march down into the Woleb and get them myself, and things can all go back to the way they were before."

"Oh, I'm 'fraid you can't be doin' that," said Guff, sounding a little more serious than he had so far. "You see, kidderling, your grown-ups aren't quite the same as you remember 'em."

The Creakers started giggling, which sounded more like the way you gargle when you brush your teeth.

"What . . . what do you mean?" Lucy said, starting to

get a little panicked. "What have you done to them?"

"We?" said Scratch. "Not we! Not us little Creakers, not Grunt, Guff, Scratch, and Sniff. We's be good little Creakers. We's not hurtin' your—"

"Grown-ups," jumped in Sniff.

"Then *who*?" asked Lucy, her mind racing to work out this riddle.

"It be the Woleb," said Grunt darkly. "The Woleb doin' what the Woleb does."

"What *does* the Woleb do?" asked Lucy.

The Creakers looked at each other with wicked smiles.

"The Woleb be changin' 'em," said Grunt.

"The Woleb be twistin' 'em," said Guff.

"The Woleb be keepin' 'em . . . ," added Scratch.

"Forever," whispered Sniff.

CHAPTER THIRTEEN

. . . Hang on! Isn't thirteen an unlucky number? It feels a little bit reckless to be writing a book about creepy creatures that live under your bed and then just whack in an unlucky chapter number like it's no big deal. What if you read this chapter and then a Creaker snatched you? I'd feel so guilty! Shall we skip straight to Chapter Fourteen? I think it's probably wise. You never can be too careful where Creakers are concerned.

Chapter Fourteen
HUMAN SPELLS

Lucy couldn't hold it together any longer. She'd been staying strong ever since the day it all began. She'd already lost her dad. Now hearing these creatures say that she might never get her mom back too was just too much.

So Lucy did the only thing a person can do when there's nothing more a person can do.

She had a good old cry.

She howled and wailed, sitting on top of the laundry basket with the four hideous Creakers trapped underneath, listening to her sobs. The tears started filling up the insides of her swimming goggles, but she didn't dare

take them off. She definitely didn't trust the Creakers.

"What's the kidder doin'?" said Scratch.

"What a rotten noise!" said Sniff, plugging his floppy ears with his long fingers.

"I'm . . . crying . . . you . . . horrid . . . things," Lucy sobbed.

"Cryin'? What is cryin'?" Sniff asked, and out of the corner of her teary eyes Lucy could see all four Creakers peering up at her through the bars of the laundry basket.

"Haven't you ever seen anyone cry before?" Lucy sniffed.

"No," the Creakers said together.

"We be creakin' when kidders are a-snoozin'. We never seen a cryin' human befores," explained Grunt.

Lucy wiped away the tears that trickled down her cheeks and sniffed up a sob.

"Well, crying is what you do when you're really, really sad about something," she said.

"Cryin' is bad?" Guff asked eagerly. "Us Creakers usually be likin' the bad stuff!"

"Actually, my dad used to say that crying is a good thing. It's when all the sad stuff inside your mind builds up so much that it starts to leak out of your eyes. It's good to let it out," said Lucy.

The Creakers went quiet beneath her, like they were really thinking about what she'd just said.

"Sometimes I thinks I might have *too* much bad stuff inside my noggin," admitted Scratch, peeling a bit of skin from his itchy scalp and popping it into his mouth.

Human Spells

"Every night it's creakin' here and creakin' there. Snatchin' grown-ups one day, dozyin' kidders the next . . ." His voice started to sound rather strange, almost like he was trying not to laugh.

"I knows what you mean," said Sniff, who started giggling a little.

"All we be doin' is the nasties, night in and night out!" agreed Guff.

And with that, the three of them cracked up in fits of laughter.

Lucy stared down at them. *What horrible creatures,* she thought. *Laughing at someone who's upset!*

But then she remembered that these Creakers were from a *backward* world—and that when they laughed, it actually sounded like crying. So did this mean that now that they were laughing they were actually upset? It was all very confusing and rather odd.

"Pull yourselves together, you twozzles," hissed Grunt. "The kidderling be puttin' you under kidderling spells, makin' you all humany and washy-brained. Naughty human magic!" He glared up at Lucy through the bars of the laundry basket.

"I'm not putting them under spells!" protested Lucy. "I don't know any spells at all. Humans can't do magic! I just told you a story, that's all."

"Exactly. Stories *are* magic. They puts ideas in your noggin that weren't in there before. They makes you think all different 'bout the world," barked Grunt grumpily, and the other Creakers snapped out of Lucy's story spell and came back to their rotten senses.

All of a sudden something seemed to happen that made the Creakers shift awkwardly. Their wrinkly ears pricked up like a cat hearing a mouse squeak. Then Lucy heard the church bell chime in the distance. What time was it? Lucy started counting.

"It's gettin' early!" Grunt said.

"The dark be nearly over," said Guff.

"Let's us be goin' back to the—" began Scratch.

"Woleb!" finished Sniff.

"Nope," Lucy said, tightening the straps of her goggles. She shifted around until she was comfortable on top of the basket and stared straight at them in the mirror. "You're not going anywhere until you tell me what I want to know. Why are you here and what have you done with our grown-ups?"

The church bell stopped. It was five o'clock. Almost morning.

"Tell 'er, Grunt. It's the only ways," said Guff. "We be dust if she don't let us be goin' back!"

"Dust?" Lucy asked, but the Creakers pressed their ugly lips together tightly, and she could see they weren't going to say any more. She tried again. "Tell me everything, or you're staying here!"

There was a silence as Grunt thought about what to do. He was caught in a rotten pickle . . . though actually Grunt loved rotten pickle, especially when it was in a moldy cheese sandwich. This was more like being caught in a fresh strawberry for Grunt—which he hated!

"Tell 'er, Grunt!" whispered Sniff nervously.

"Yes, Grunt," said Lucy. "Tell me what I want and I'll let you go, but I won't ask you again. *What have you done with the grown-ups?*"

"All wrong, then, Grunt be tellin' the tricksy kidderling. But Grunt be gettin' in the troubles for this," Grunt muttered.

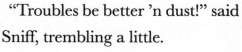

"Troubles be better 'n dust!" said Sniff, trembling a little.

Grunt sighed and ran his claws over his spiky nailed back.

"It be simply easy to understand. We Creakers, we be hatin' them stupid grown-ups," he said.

"Hating the grown-ups?" said Lucy.

"HATIN' 'em like the smell of roses on a sunny mornin'."

"Hatin' 'em like the taste of raspberry-ripple ice cream."

"Hatin' 'em like a warm 'ot-water bottle on a cold night," all the Creakers agreed, shuddering.

"But why?" asked Lucy.

"Them stupid human grown-ups be takin' all the stinkerful waste and . . . and . . ."

Lucy noticed that Grunt was getting very agitated as he tried to spit out these words.

". . . they WASTE it!" he spat.

"They waste what?"

"They waste the WASTE!" all the Creakers barked in unison.

"All the glorious garbage."

"All the rotten leftovers."

"All the stuff you silly humans use once and then get rids of, they takes it and chucks it in the watery oceans," said Grunt.

"They buries it under the ground!" added Guff.

"Or they burns it all up into smoky clouds. Hidin' it outta sight, outta brain, but worst of all, outta reach of us—"

"Creakers!" said Scratch and Sniff together.

"Right," said Lucy. "So . . . what's the problem with all that?"

The Creakers bashed their sticky hands on their slimy foreheads and let out frustrated moans.

"Innit obvious, you silly kidderling?" answered Grunt. "We Creakers don't just loves the stuff you be gettin' rids of. We *NEEDS* it."

"It's what the Woleb works on," Guff explained. "All

them things your grown-ups be thinkin' is rotten and nasty and wants outta their homes—we Creakers wants to 'ave it."

"Oh, I see! To reuse it?" said Lucy.

"YES!" they barked.

"That's why we be snatchin' up all the grown-ups, takin' them away, just leavin' the messy kidderlings behind," Grunt explained.

"You little muckers knows how to make good muck," Guff said approvingly. "And you not be clearin' it up. We be able to come and takes all the mess we wants now. We takes it back and builds stinkerful homes."

"You make homes out of garbage?" Lucy asked.

"Oh yes!" Guff said enthusiastically. "We makes the worst rotten homes in all the Woleb! Big smelly ones where the walls are made of lumpy cardboard egg boxes and the windows outta fizzywhizz bottles."

"I got a pure banana-peel rug!" said Scratch.

"And my pillows is plastic bags stuffed with empty tin cans!" boasted Sniff.

"I . . . I see," said Lucy. She tried to imagine their homes, built from the garbage she would throw in the trash can. They sounded rather awful to her, but the Creakers seemed very proud of how disgusting they were.

"So if we lets your stupid grown-ups go on hidin' it all in the ground . . . ," went on Grunt.

"Or the oceans . . ."

"Or the sky . . ."

"We be havin' nothin' to live by anymores," Guff finished. "We not be able to survive in the Woleb."

Lucy took a moment to really think about everything they'd said. She thought about all the mess she made, and where it went when her mom threw it away, and about all those truckloads of trash bags she used to see her dad drive off to Whiffington Dump each day.

"Now the kidderling be lettin' us go? Like she promised, yes?" said Grunt.

"Before the sun dusts us all!" blurted Guff.

"Be quiet, you twit!" snapped Grunt, shoving Guff so hard that Lucy felt the laundry basket wobble beneath her. "You be tellin' her our weakyness!"

"The sun . . . dusts you?" Lucy asked. Her brain was whirring. "Do you not like sunlight?"

Grunt sighed, and in the mirror Lucy saw him shoot Guff a nasty look.

"The sun be too nice," he grumbled.

"And warm."

"And loverly."

"And kind."

"Our dark green skin be too fragile to see it. That's why we live in the Woleb, under the beds. Sunlight can't gets to us down there. We be turnin' to dust if we gets caught in it," explained Sniff, reaching into his pouch and pulling out a sprinkle of Dozy Dust.

"You mean—you mean that Dozy Dust is made of . . . of . . ."

"Dusted Creaker," Sniff said sadly, placing it back in the pouch and pulling the strings tight. "That be why its magic works so good and powerful."

Lucy thought of all the times she'd had little golden crumbles in the corners of her eyes when she'd woken up. She'd never wondered what it was before—but now she suddenly had a strange, uncomfortable feeling in her tummy. That dust meant that a Creaker had lost its life. They might be rotten, nasty-looking things, but Lucy was

168

beginning to think that they actually weren't all that bad.

"Look! It be the bright!" cried Guff, pointing his flabby claw to the sliver of warm orange light that had just crept in through Lucy's curtains.

Their time was up!

Chapter Fifteen
BACK TO THE WOLEB!

H as your mom or dad ever burned the dinner? Or maybe a piece of toast at breakfast time?

Do you remember what it smelled like?

It's horrible, isn't it?

Well, that very same smell suddenly wafted up Lucy's nostrils.

"HOT! HOT! HOT!" the Creakers cried as the first pools of wonderful morning sunlight reached the basket they were trapped in and cut through the bars like knives. Lucy looked down and gasped as she saw their skin puffing up like bubbling molasses at the first drop of light.

"Lets us go!" Grunt growled.

Back to the Woleb!

"Oh my goodness! I'm sorry!" Lucy said, leaping from the basket at once. She lifted it off the four Creakers and rushed to the curtains to draw them closed, buying the creatures some time.

But when she turned back around, her heart thumped in her chest. The Creakers were tugging her dad's grubby coat off Ella's floppy sleeping body.

"Hey! That's my dad's!" cried Lucy.

"Stupid little kidderling. Never trust a Creaker!" Grunt cried as he put the coat on himself, wearing it like a royal robe. Then, in a split second, he slid underneath Lucy's bed, much faster than Lucy had seen the Creakers move before. Guff, Scratch, and Sniff followed, giggling and laughing in their weird, twisted way as they slipped into the blackness below.

"No!" Lucy cried—but it was too late. They had gone, along with her dad's coat, back to their backward Woleb!

She quickly shook Ella. "Wake up, you sleepyhead!"

"But . . . but I only like the pink marshmallows . . . ," Ella mumbled in her dreamy voice.

Lucy jumped onto her bed, bouncing up and down and shaking Norman.

"Wake up, you useless boy!" she called. "There's no Scout badge for *sleeping-through-a-crisis!*"

Actually, there is *a Scout badge for* sleeping-through-a-crisis. *It looks like this . . .*

It was hopeless. Norman and Ella were too heavily under the Dozy Dust's magic to be woken. Lucy was on her own—and she had to think quickly.

Back to the Woleb!

"That's right. I've got to think quickly," Lucy told herself firmly. "I'm the only person who knows where the grown-ups are and how to get there. I've got to find Mom. I've got to get her back!"

Lucy dropped to the floor and peered into the dark space beneath her bed. The wooden boards appeared to be normal, but Lucy knew better now. She reached out slowly and prodded one with her fingertips.

The floor wobbled!

The wormhole to the Woleb was still open! But as Lucy thought this, the floor gave a little shake, and a bubble rose to the surface and popped, as though it were some sort of living jelly. Lucy pulled her hand back quickly and felt the warmth of the morning sun as it illuminated her room through the thin curtains.

The sunlight must be making the wormhole close! thought Lucy. *That's it—it's now or never.*

She pulled the straps of her swimming goggles tight, pushed her bangs to one side, took a deep breath, and slid headfirst into the shadows beneath her bed.

The floor swallowed her up whole. In an instant, she

sank into the squashy-swishy, wobbly-bobbly floor—she was back in the Woleb once more.

Lucy tried to relax, to let the sticky walls tighten and stretch around her and finally spit her out into the strange Woleb tunnel. She flipped upside down, or was it downside up? Either way, she felt awfully dizzy again as she toppled onto her bottom next to the hole that led to her bedroom.

Suddenly the hole started to glow a glorious orange, like a warm sunrise, before shrinking and disappearing completely.

"The wormhole must close in the daytime and stop sunlight from getting in, protecting the Creakers and the Woleb from being *dusted*," Lucy murmured. "But that also means . . . I can't get out! I'm stuck down here now—at least until it's nighttime in Whiffington again."

A Creaker laugh echoed down the steamy corridor, and Lucy saw four twisted shadows scurry off in the distance.

BACK TO THE WOLEB!

"We gots the stinkerful jacket!" she heard Grunt cackle.

"Scratch be usin' it as a duvet to sleep in."

"Sniff wants it as a rotten rug!"

"Guff be makin' a pair of whiffy coat curtains with it."

"None of yous be 'avin' this stinkin' thing. We be takin' it to the king!" Grunt hissed.

"The king?" Lucy whispered to herself.

"All hails the king!" the Creakers snapped in unison as they marched deeper into the tunnel.

The King of the Creakers. He must be the worst of all of them! Lucy thought.

And she was right. The Creaker King was the worst Creaker in all the Woleb—but even worse than that, what Lucy didn't yet know was that to rescue the grown-ups and to get her mom back, Lucy was going to have to face him . . .

Don't tell her!

Chapter Sixteen

THE MARSHMALLOW OF YOUR DREAMS

The campfire was warm and cozy, and the smell of toasting marshmallows made Norman's tummy rumble with excitement.

He twisted his marshmallow around in the flickering orange flames, getting the most perfectly even toast you could possibly imagine. This one didn't look black and charred like they usually did, and it didn't go all sloppy and fall off his stick. It was golden and crisp. It was warm and bubbling. It was, quite simply, the sort of toasted marshmallow you only see in your dreams.

Which is exactly where it was. In Norman's dream.

Suddenly his cozy little campfire was interrupted by

the most irritating sound Norman had ever heard. It was like a siren wailing through the sky, filling the air with annoyance.

OORRRAAAA OOOOORRRRRRAAAARRRR OOOOOORRRAAAAA

"What on earth is that sound?" Norman cried, dropping his marshmallow into the flames to cover his ears as the sound got louder.

OOOORRRRMAAAAA

OOOOORRRRRRMAAAAA

NOOOOORRRRMAAAA

NOOOORMAAAAN!

NOOORMAAAN!

NORMAN!

Norman sat upright in Lucy's bed.

"Norman? It's me, Ella!" Ella called, looking all scruffy and tired.

"I fell asleep?" Norman croaked.

"Guess so. We both did!"

"You fell asleep too?"

"Uh-huh." Ella yawned, popping on her pink heart-shaped shades to hide her tired eyes from the crack of sunlight coming in through the curtains, making Lucy's bedroom glow.

"Where's the jacket?" Norman asked, noticing that Ella was no longer wearing Lucy's dad's coat.

"Dunno," Ella said with a shrug. "Woke up and it was gone."

The Marshmallow of Your Dreams

Norman's brain was only just warming up. He couldn't work anything out yet.

He caught Ella's yawn and rubbed his eyes. That's when he noticed the little golden crumbles of sleep fall onto the bedsheets. The little speckles that had been in the corners of his eyes.

His heart leapt.

"Lucy!" he gasped.

"She's not in there," Ella said as Norman scrambled out of bed and stumbled across to the wardrobe.

"She's—"

"Gone?" Ella interrupted.

Norman nodded.

"She's probably just downstairs making breakfast."

"No, Ella—you don't understand. They've snatched her!"

Ella dipped her head and peered over the top of her sunglasses with a raised eyebrow.

"Who?"

"The Creakers! They must have snatched her in the night once we fell asleep!" Norman whispered.

"Snatched? Really?" Ella questioned, seeming rather unconvinced.

"REALLY! I guess the first part of the plan must have worked."

"Plan? What plan?" Ella asked.

Norman suddenly realized he'd better not tell Ella that they had only invited her in order to use her as live bait to lure a bunch of creepy monsters out in the hope of catching them.

"Well?" Ella said, tapping her foot impatiently.

"Ella, those dreams you had . . ."

"The ones about the monsters under my bed?"

"Exactly! Those weren't dreams, Ella. They were real. *They* are real."

"Who?" Ella said.

Norman raised a shaky finger, pointing at the shadows under Lucy's bed.

"The Creakers," Ella jumped in again as she started to realize what was going on and just how serious the situation had become. "We need the grown-ups," she said.

"We need Lucy!" said Norman.

OK, we're about to dive down into the Woleb with Lucy. Are you ready? You might want to go to the bathroom before reading this chapter. I'd hate for you to have a little accident. No? OK, don't say I didn't warn you. By reading on, you agree that the author accepts no responsibility for any toilet-related mishaps you may have as a result of being scared by the following chapter(s).

Chapter Seventeen
YOU'RE NOT HERE!

Lucy crept along the creepy, stinky corridor, following the wretched voices of Guff, Grunt, Scratch, and Sniff as they creaked deeper into the Woleb.

She stepped over the little wooden signs, reading the names of all her Whiffington neighbors, and her tummy gave a little flutter as she thought of all the children above, waking up to another grown-up-less day, not knowing anything about this place, not realizing what was at stake.

Of course, Lucy knew exactly what was at stake. And you know too.

You're Not Here!

If Lucy couldn't find the grown-ups, if she got lost down here, she might never find her way out, and the children of Whiffington would never see their families again.

Suddenly a second corridor appeared in front of her, one she was sure hadn't been there a moment ago. She scratched her head as she stared at the fork in the road and the choice she now had to make. Should she go left? Or right? Or should she take the third tunnel?

The third tunnel?

Where did that come from? Lucy thought. *That* definitely *wasn't there a moment ago.*

She glanced back the way she had come—and stared in disbelief.

It was now a dead end!

The Woleb was changing.

It was moving!

Like it was *alive.*

Lucy felt crushed.

"I'm never going to be able to find my way around here. This is impossible!" she said, and slumped to the sticky floor in a huff.

As those words came out of her mouth, they felt so strange. She'd never said that anything was impossible before. She usually hated those words.

Her mom's voice suddenly popped into her head: *Impossible isn't real. It's just in your mind.*

Lucy's heart sank. It meant that down here, in this backward place, impossible was very real.

Impossible.

Mind.

Lucy's head went fuzzy—and then her thoughts suddenly became crystal clear, as though her mind was an old TV and someone had just tuned it properly.

"Wait a second. If the thing I'm trying to do—rescue the grown-ups from nasty monsters—*IS* impossible . . . then down in the Woleb, where everything is what it isn't . . . it is totally **POSSIBLE**!" she cried. "It's the one place in the world where I *can* do this!"

Lucy jumped back to her feet. She'd had an idea.

"I know exactly where I'm going," she announced as loudly as she could, her voice echoing down the multiple tunnels and hallways that had appeared around her. "I don't need a MAP! The last thing I would ever want is a precise, detailed map of the entire Woleb. If anything, a MAP would just slow me down."

Lucy waited hopefully. There was a deep silence. She peered down each of the twisted routes ahead of her as they wound deeper into this weird world.

Then, all of a sudden, something caught her eye. Something stuck to the wall of one of the tunnels. She ran over to it, her heart skipping in her chest. It was a giant map spread out on the wall, like the ones you see in shopping malls.

Lucy grinned. Her plan had worked! She had tricked the Woleb!

"Oh no, not a map!" she said out loud. "This isn't helpful at all . . ."

Lucy took a step closer to get a better look at the map. She thought her swimming goggles might be playing tricks on her, so she lifted them up to check, but . . . nope. The map was unlike any Lucy had ever seen before.

It looked like this:

It looked like Whiffington Town, but sliced in half, like an apple. Underneath the town there were no layers of rock or a hot lava core, like Lucy was used to seeing in the maps of the earth in her earth science lessons at school. Instead, there was a complicated network of tunnels winding downward into the ground—tunnels that led to a large Creaker city.

Lucy gasped. It was unbelievable. If you stood back, it looked like an enormous black spider was living somewhere inside the planet, with all its legs poking up to the surface—a secret monster beneath all the homes in Whiffington.

She leaned in to take an even closer look . . .

And the spider suddenly moved.

"AHHHH!" Lucy cried.

The Woleb *was* alive! As the spider on the map stretched and shifted one of its knobbly legs, Lucy heard a great creak from the tunnel ahead of her and saw the entire thing bend and stretch before settling down, now leading to a new location. No wonder all these tunnels appeared out of nowhere. This whole world was moving. Changing.

You're Not Here!

Lucy took a breath and leaned in again. Now she could read some of the locations in the Creaker city.

There was a public swimming pool filled with live rats and cockroaches . . .

A restaurant serving leftover brussels sprouts from Christmases past. The most expensive sprout on the menu was one found in a garbage can at Buckingham Palace in 1953, which had been severely undercooked and partially chewed, possibly by royalty. Possibly not.

There were shops selling stinky old shoes with holes in them . . .

Shops selling stinky old socks to match the stinky old shoes . . .

Shops selling ice cream, which was actually scoops of human earwax . . .

Shops selling belly-button-fluff blankets . . .

A market with only rotten vegetables . . .

A lumpy river of spoiled milk . . .

And just about every gross thing that Lucy could imagine. Actually, this place was so gross that a nice girl like Lucy wouldn't even have been able to imagine it.

As Lucy scanned the map, she noticed a small red dot

with an arrow pointing to it. Above it were the words
YOU'RE NOT HERE.

Lucy smiled to herself. She knew it meant that this
was *exactly* where she was. She was beginning to figure
out this backward place.

"This map is so unhelpful. But what would be even
less useful would be to know where the grown-ups are
being kept. I definitely don't want to know that!" she
said loudly, and waited.

Suddenly a great hole opened up in the wall to her
right, like giant tree roots twisting themselves open. A
new spider's leg appeared on the map next to the spot
where she was. She traced it with her finger to see where
it led, and her tummy did a little flip when she reached
the end. There was a picture of what looked like a fairground on the map, with these words written above it:

CREAKERLAND
THE NO-FUNFAIR

You're Not Here!

Suddenly a scream echoed through the new opening, which gave Lucy the chills.

Because it wasn't a Creaker screaming . . .

It was a grown-up.

Chapter Eighteen
THE BOG TAVERN

Grunt, Guff, Scratch, and Sniff creaked through the Woleb, carrying Mr. Dungston's stinking coat.

"His Rottenness be awful pleased with Grunt when he sniffs this," said Grunt.

"And Guff," said Guff.

"And Scr—" began Scratch.

"And Sniff!" added Sniff happily. "Sorry, Scratch," he quickly added.

They all wound their way through the crooked, winding, twisted tunnels, deeper into their backward world.

"Shall we stops off on the ways for snacks?" asked Guff hopefully, rubbing his rumbling round belly.

"No, you flabby rotbag! We be gettin' this to His Rottenness rights aways," Grunt barked.

"But, Grunt, we's be 'avin' a long night wot with that crafty kidderling. We at least deserves some sludge," Guff pleaded, giving Scratch a little nudge.

"Oh yeah, some old sludge would go down a trick," Scratch agreed.

"All wrong, all wrong! We stops for a quickybit, but just one slop," Grunt said sternly, caving in to the demands of Guff's greedy belly.

They turned a sharp left (which went right) and almost walked straight into the wall of the tunnel, but just as their pointed noses were about to bash into it, a brand-new hole twisted open. Entwined tree roots and mud cracked apart, and a new path was revealed.

As they creaked through the hole, a great raucous sound filled the new tunnel. It came from a building in the distance. I say a building, but it was more like a pile of bricks, rubble, smashed glass, and bent steel that might have once been a building but had long since

been demolished. Swinging from the top of the ruin was a bent, rusty old sign, which read **THE BOG TAVERN.** The Creakers had banded together to bring this whole derelict building site down into the Woleb, and it was now the place they all went to have a slop or two of sludge after a long night of creaking.

The Bog Tavern was always busy. As they stepped through the doorless doorway, the glorious stench of damp and mold filled their snotty nostrils, and they heard a discordant song from the Creaker playing a strange, creaky instrument in the corner. It had the bashed-up keys of an old piano, the dented horn of a trombone, three bent pipes from some bagpipes, one broken guitar string, and a little triangle on top, all cobbled together into one.

"Oh looks, they gots Belch playin' the bogpipes tonight. 'E's awful, 'e is. Can't play a single note wrong!" Guff said, rubbing his claws together gleefully. He loved the Bog Tavern.

Grunt trudged to the bar, and a respectful hush fell over the rotten room as every stinking Creaker in the place realized who had just set claw inside.

"What'll it be, Grunt?" barked Squelch, the landlord, breaking the silence.

"Four slops," Grunt replied. "And make 'em quicks. We gots important business."

"And some pork rinds!" Guff added to the order, followed by one of his stinky butt-puffs.

"Wrong away. Anythin' for the king's most untrusted Creakers," Squelch muttered with a dip of his bald, scabby head.

They made their way through the crowds of Creakers who were busy sharing creaking stories.

"I nearly gots dusted last night," one old Creaker called Bulge said as he gulped the last mouthful of sludge from his glass. "Chubby kidderling fell outta bed and landed on me. I broke the rotten thing's fall so it didn't wake up, see? So there I was, trapped with this heavy lump of a kidder on me leg—and then the bright started comin'!"

"What did y' do, Bulge?" asked Barf, the wrinkly Creaker sharing his table.

"Had to gnaw me own leg off, didn't I!" And with that, Bulge plunked his dark green leg on the table,

and all the Creakers who were listening cheered and clinked their goblets together in celebration. Everyone loved it when a Creaker escaped being dusted. "I'll stick it back on somehow!" Bulge laughed.

"Bunch of twitnits," Grunt huffed grumpily as he and Guff found space at an empty table. Scratch and Sniff made their way to join Belch on the bogpipes and began singing along to all the songs they didn't know.

"You're always rotten in the face when you comes in here," Guff said to Grunt as he perched his bottom on an upturned stool.

"Look at 'em all. All these useless lumps of Creaky flesh. Wastin' away their hours in here, tellin' nonsense waffle to each other."

"It's just whats we do, Grunt," Guff said.

"Not me. Not Grunt," Grunt whispered. "I be wantin' more."

Guff stared. "More? More 'n what?"

"More 'n *Creakin'*," said Grunt. "It always be the same. Sneakin' up there into the human world, where everythin's the right way up. Stealin' their garbage, night in and night out. Never gettin' to see my Creakerlings back home." He pulled out a little photo of his hideously ugly Creaker children to show Guff.

"Ahh, they gets more disgustin' every year," Guff said politely.

"Thanks, I know. Just likes their mother." Grunt sighed fondly at the photo before tucking it away.

"But this be the Creaker way, Grunt. Creakin' is what we does. It puts muck on the table and mulch over our 'eads," Guff said.

"Have you never thoughts in your noggin what it might be like *not* 'avin' to creak abouts? *Not* 'avin' to do the nasties up there? *Not* stealin' things that isn't ours?" Grunt replied in a hushed voice.

"Four quick slops," interrupted Squelch before Guff could answer, spilling most of their sludge on the table as he put their overflowing goblets down. "Made 'em just the way you like, Grunt. Rotten eggs, cheese flakes, broccoli juice, and I put some extra snot drops in for you tonight too. On the house," Squelch added as he wiped his nose.

"Cheers." Guff grinned, stuffing the whole bag of pork rinds in his mouth—including the foil wrapping.

"Cheers," Grunt muttered, and made to take a swig of his sludge. But before the chipped glass touched his cracked lips, the whole building site around them began to rumble.

The rumble became a shake.

The shake became a jolting **Wolebquake!**
Broken bricks broke again and fell to the ground.

Slops of sludge smashed and spilled. The cracked glass in the windows shattered completely.

"Takes cover!" ordered Grunt as he dived on top of Lucy's dad's stinking jacket to protect it.

The rumbling slowly calmed down. The shaking settled. The Wolebquake was over, and the whole Bog Tavern was silent in shock.

"What the muck was that, Grunt?" grumbled Squelch the landlord as he climbed out from under his bar.

Grunt got to his feet, brushing debris from the precious, stinking coat.

"*That,*" he replied grimly, "is a kidderling in the Woleb."

CHAPTER NINETEEN
CREAKERLAND

Lucy sprinted down the tunnel, following it deeper into the Woleb. The screams were growing louder with every step she took.

She rounded a crooked corner and the spider-leg tunnel opened up into a great cave, stretching out far above her head where the roots of trees poked through mud and dirt. The sticky ground beneath her feet suddenly became a row of neat, polished green paving stones, and this path led down to something so strange Lucy had to take off her swimming goggles to get a good look at it.

Right in front of her eyes was a ginormous

underground theme park. It was massive! Bigger than any fairground or theme park Lucy had ever seen.

Farther along the path was a giant entrance with bright, shiny turnstiles and a curly-swirly sign over the top that said:

WELCOME TO
CREAKERLAND
THE NO-FUNFAIR

Where dreams definitely don't come true

The most miserable place below the earth

But Lucy knew that in the Woleb this meant it *was* a fun place. A place where dreams *do* come true.

"But whose dreams?" Lucy asked herself quietly so the Woleb wouldn't hear her thoughts.

Her mind was interrupted by the screams again as

the carriages of an enormous roller coaster whizzed by and did a huge loop-the-loop high up over her head, the track skimming the cavernous, rooty roof above. The seats of the roller coaster were packed with passengers dressed in their pajamas and nighties, all waving their hands high above their heads.

And that's when Lucy realized two things.

The passengers in the roller-coaster cars were all grown-ups.

And it was these grown-ups who were screaming— but they weren't screaming in pain or fear. They were screaming with laughter and happiness.

Lucy saw their faces as the roller coaster shot by. They were giddy with excitement, wide childish smiles stretched across their faces as they waved their arms in the air.

What the jiggins?! thought Lucy as she rushed down the shiny green path to the turnstile and gave it a push. It spun around and whacked her on the bottom, shoving her into Creakerland.

She was suddenly hit by the most delicious, sweet smell. Lucy closed her eyes and breathed it in deeply. It

205

was the smell of sugar and caramel, freshly baked cookies, and steaming hot chocolate. It was the nicest thing she'd smelled since being down here, and it seemed completely out of place in this rotten world.

As she looked around, she couldn't believe what she was seeing. There were rides and roller coasters that looked so mind-bogglingly fun that she found herself being drawn toward them, desperately wanting to ride them. Some had stomach-churning twists soaring so high it hurt her neck to keep looking at them.

There was a merry-go-round that whizzed around so fast and didn't stop until the grown-ups riding it couldn't hold on any longer. They just let go, flying into the sky, landing in huge piles of pink fluff.

"Cotton candy!" Lucy whispered in amazement as she watched the grown-ups eat their way out of these pink fluffy piles of deliciousness, which were as tall as the houses of Whiffington.

There were popcorn machines on the rooftops of all the buildings, continuously popping fresh, buttery popcorn, which burst into the air and fell like warm, delicious popcorn-snow over their heads.

A large pink milkshake river flowed around a silver castle in the center of it all. Lucy rubbed her eyes and saw that the castle was in fact made of hundreds and thousands of sparkling silver garbage cans, stacked high on top of one another.

"Wow!" Lucy said out loud. This place really was strangely amazing. She couldn't help but want to dive into the milkshake river and go for a swim with her mouth wide open.

Two women skipped by, holding hands, eating enormous lollipops, and giggling like little kids as they played in the falling popcorn, trying to catch it on their tongues.

"Excuse me!" Lucy called to them, but the women turned and blew raspberries at her, then ran away laughing. As Lucy watched them go, a crowd of men burst out of a toy shop, kicking a brand-new football.

"On yer head!" one of them called, and toe-punted the ball so hard it smashed through the shop window, showering the street with glass. The men fell about laughing.

"Nice one, Simon!" another man said. "Let's drink some cream soda and go on the rides until we puke again!"

Lucy, who didn't usually consider puking very funny,

found that a little giggle was making its way out of her mouth.

"Oh!" she said, taking herself by surprise.

Just then, a great blast of trumpets broke out from the far end of Main Street, Creakerland. "Oooh, it's a parade!" cried an elderly man next to Lucy, beaming and turning a cartwheel as a row of giant floats began cruising their way down the street.

Crowds of all the grown-ups of Whiffington suddenly emerged from the Main Street shops and attractions—the video-game arcade, the ice-cream spa, the comic-book library, the hot-fudge hot tub, and the petting zoo—filling the street to watch. Wrinkly Mr. Ratcliffe was there in his underpants. Molly the milk woman was handing out Woleb milkshakes, and even Mario was jogging backward along Main Street.

Then Lucy spotted Mrs. Fudge McScroodles, who owned Scrummy McScroodles Sweets 'n' Stuff; Old Man Carvey, who ran the butcher shop; Paige Turner, the librarian; and even Piers Snoregan from *Wakey-Wakey, Whiffington*. They were all here in Creakerland—having fun in their pajamas!

The grown-ups whooped and cheered as the parade came past, as though they were having the time of their lives. It *was* fun—but Lucy couldn't help but feel that this was all wrong. These childlike people around her were the grown-ups who should be up in Whiffington with their children and families. Not down here.

Lucy turned away, her mind racing. A woman with curly white hair skipped past her, holding a large ice cream. The chocolate was melting in her hands, making them sticky and messy. The woman tossed the melting ice cream on the ground, and it landed with a splodge right at Lucy's feet.

"Excuse me, aren't you going to clean that up?" Lucy asked.

The woman's expression changed from a sort of hypnotic excitement to utter hysterics.

"Clean it up?! Pah-ha-ha!" she called. "Good one! I'm off to get a fresh ice cream. Want one?"

As much as Lucy would have loved an ice cream, she knew that there was some sort of Woleb magic at work here, and magical ice cream was not to be trusted. "No thanks," she replied, and watched the old woman run full speed down Main Street to the ice-cream vending machine, faster than a kid running downstairs on Christmas morning.

As the woman disappeared, another grown-up came into view. Lucy stared at the distant figure. Then, as she realized what she was seeing, she clapped her hands over her eyes and peered through her fingers. It was an awful sight, which she was afraid she could never un-see. It was Ella's father, the mayor of Whiffington—and he wasn't wearing any clothes. At. All.

Lucy groaned as Mayor Noying, who was usually very serious indeed, ran down Main Street—completely naked. He was covering up his funny bits with a ridiculous Creakerland mayor's hat, screaming, "I'm mayor of Creakerland, and I declare this the BEST PLACE EV-ER!" at the top of his lungs.

Lucy quickly shut her eyes tightly as his

bare bottom whizzed past her and disappeared down Main Street.

"I couldn't agree more!" said Piers Snoregan as his film crew captured the mayor's naked moment. "That's about all from me, Piers Snoregan. See you tomorrow for another *Wakey-Wakey, Woleb.*" He winked smugly at the camera before the broadcast ended, and the film crew high-fived each other.

"I'm *never* telling Ella about this," Lucy muttered to herself.

She stared at the chaos around her. *What the jiggins is going on?* she wondered. *Why are all the grown-ups acting so . . . so . . .*

And just like that, she understood why the grown-ups weren't acting like grown-ups anymore. It was all so blindingly obvious that Lucy slicked her hair over and slapped herself on the forehead for not realizing it sooner.

Of course! she thought. *This is the twisted work of the Woleb again!*

Everything in this place was different. It was backward. And the grown-ups were no exception.

Because the grown-ups *weren't* grown-ups down here. They were naughty and silly and fun—like *children.*

And most important of all, they were messy!

Lucy looked around at all the litter on the ground. There were candy wrappers, greasy french fry bags, lollipop sticks, bottles, and cans. There were scattered jelly beans and drips of chocolate. There were bits of broken glass and piles of discarded popcorn. There was litter EVERYWHERE!

Just what the Creakers wanted, Lucy realized.

The grown-ups had been snatched away into the Woleb and had forgotten about their lives. This place had erased their responsibilities. It had made them forget all the stresses and worries of the *real* world and remember instead what it was like to be children: to simply have fun. A life without consequence.

It was only then that Lucy realized the true meaning of the word she hated. *Impossible.* How was she ever going to fix this mess?

"Impossible is just in your mind. Impossible is just in your mind," Lucy repeated to herself.

At that moment, she heard a laugh she recognized,

213

and spun around. She looked down the glistening green-paved street and saw a giddy girl tumble out of the exit of the Tilt-A-Whirl, fall to the shiny floor, and begin rolling around in a fit of giddy giggles.

"Let's do it again!" she said, laughing.

Lucy stared.

It was her mom.

Chapter Twenty
NORMELLATRON

"This is a disaster! We're all doomed!" Ella whined, flopping onto Lucy's pillow dramatically.

Norman paced around the room behind her, his feet squeaking on the creaky floorboards in rhythm.

"Not necessarily," he said.

"Oh please, Norman. It's useless. Mama and Papa are gone. Lucy's gone. There are monsters under our beds, and . . . yep, there are only white marshmallows left." Ella inspected the half-empty bag. "This is the worst day of my life. I officially quit."

"Lucy wouldn't quit on us," insisted Norman. "She didn't give up on the grown-ups."

215

Ella sighed. "OK, Mr. Scouty-Pants with all the badges. What do we do, then?"

Norman closed his eyes and thought as hard as he could. "What would Lucy do?"

They both sat there in Lucy's bedroom, wondering what Lucy would do if she woke up and found out that *she* was missing. What would Lucy Dungston do if—

"Wait a second," Ella said, interrupting the narrator. "We already know what Lucy would do."

"We do?"

"Yuh-huh! She already did it . . . when the grown-ups first disappeared!"

Norman scratched his neatly combed head, trying to remember.

"She put on her school uniform?" he guessed.

"No! Don't you remember what she said? *How did my mom find out what was going on in the world?*" Ella said in her best Lucy voice.

Norman's eyes lit up. "The news!"

"Right! You know what? We just worked all that out together. We're a team now, Norm. We've got to stick together," Ella said.

"Yeah! Like two Transformers coming together to build an even bigger, even better one!" Norman agreed excitedly, linking his fingers together to demonstrate. "Norman and Ella. Together, we are . . . NormEllaTron!" he boomed.

This time it was Ella who scratched her head.

Slowly.

"Too much?" asked Norman nervously.

"Too much, Norm. Let's just go and switch the TV on," she said.

"OK."

They both ran downstairs, Norman switched on the TV—and together they began searching for news on Lucy.

CHAPTER TWENTY-ONE
LUCY IN CREAKERLAND

"**M**om!" Lucy called out across Main Street, Creakerland. But her call was completely ignored—not just by her mom but by every misbehaving grown-up around.

She ran straight over to her mom and helped her to her feet. She stared at her. Her mom's usually neat brown curls were frizzed and tangled, and her pajamas were crumpled and splodged with what looked like strawberry ice cream.

"That was SO much fun. You've got to try it! Let's go!" Mrs. Dungston cried, tugging on Lucy's arm as she tried to ride the vomit-inducing Tilt-A-Whirl again.

219

"Erm, I think you've had enough of that for one day," Lucy said.

"Yes, *Mommy*!" said Lucy's mom, mocking Lucy for being so bossy.

"Don't call me that."

"Don't call me that!" Mrs. Dungston repeated.

"Stop it!"

"Stop it!"

"It's not funny."

"It's not funny!"

"Why are you being so annoying?"

"Why are you being so annoying?!"

"I'm not annoying—you are!"

"I'm not annoying—you are!"

Lucy folded her arms and let out a frustrated sigh.

Her mom was acting like a spoiled child.

"OK, I'm a big snot muffin!" Lucy said.

Mrs. Dungston burst into uncontrollable giggles, pointing and laughing.

"You're a big snot muffin, you're a big snot muffin!" she sang merrily.

Lucy looked with worry at this grown woman in front of her, this lady who looked like her mom.

"What has this place done to you?" she whispered.

"Oh, lighten up, grumpy pants! It's just a bit of fun," Mrs. Dungston said, poking Lucy in the ribs.

But this wasn't fun, not for Lucy, not one bit. In fact, it was as far from fun as possible. Can you imagine your mom or dad pointing at you and saying, *"You're a big snot muffin"*? It might even make you want to cry.

Which is exactly what Lucy did.

Big-snot-muffin tears welled up in her big-snot-muffin eyes and plopped out in massive drops down her cheeks. She sobbed so hard she couldn't even see. Everything was too much. Too out of control. Too overwhelmingly stressful. All these responsibilities had fallen on Lucy's shoulders so suddenly she didn't even know where to begin. Saving the grown-ups, looking after the

Whiffington kids, confiscating dangerous items, trying to keep the place tidy. Was this what being a grown-up felt like?

Maybe the Woleb is changing me too, Lucy thought suddenly. *If this place is making the grown-ups more childlike, then isn't it possible that it's making me more grown up?*

She shook her head angrily. "If this is what being a grown-up feels like, then no thank you very much!" she cried. "Being a grown-up is terrible!"

Just then she felt a hand on her face: a kind, warm hand, wiping away the big-snot-muffin tears. Once the tears cleared, Lucy's heart seemed to melt a little at what she saw. Her mom was staring right at her, a look of astonishment on her face.

"Mom?" Lucy said.

"My little Lucypops!" said Mrs. Dungston, sounding like the woman Lucy knew.

"What happened?!" Lucy asked, wondering why her mom had suddenly woken from the strange Woleb magic.

"I . . . I can't really explain it!" Mrs. Dungston said, scratching her head. "One minute I was feeling all excited about riding these roller coasters, and then I heard something—something that made everything else seem unimportant."

"What was it?"

"You!" Mrs. Dungston said.

"But I was calling you and trying to speak to you, Mom!"

"Really? I don't remember that! I just remember hearing you crying. It's a sound that's always made me so unhappy, ever since you were tiny," Mrs. Dungston said, pulling Lucy in for an enormous, squishy cuddle. "Lucy . . ."

"Yes, Mom?"

"Where on earth are we?"

Mrs. Dungston gazed around at the mayhem surrounding them. Grown-ups were sprinting about carelessly, screaming at the tops of their voices and generally being as un-grown-up-like as they could be.

"Actually, Mom, we're not anywhere *on* earth. We're *below* it!" Lucy said, and quickly tried to explain all that she had learned about the Woleb and the Creakers who lived there. "That's why I'm here," she finished. "I've come to take everyone back home. If you think *this* place is bad, wait until you see what the kids have done to Whiffington!"

"Oh no! What's happened?" Mrs. Dungston asked.

Lucy took a deep breath.

"Well, there are three sharks in the Whiffington pool, thanks to Jackson Gilly; Billy Noshling's been stuck in a vending machine for two days; Ella and Norman have been knocked out by Dozy Dust; and, as a whole, Whiffington is pretty much a hazard to the health of anyone who sets foot in it," Lucy explained.

"What about my son?" said a worried voice from behind her. "James Crackney?"

Lucy whirled around and came face to face with an anxious-looking man in polka-dot pajamas, who appeared to have bits of cotton candy stuck in his beard. She couldn't believe it. Had another grown-up snapped out of the Creakers' spell too?

"And my daughter Suzanne? I think she's in your class . . . ," said a woman in a stripy nightie, stepping toward Lucy.

Lucy looked around and realized that a handful of

grown-ups had started listening to her. As she described the awful mess Whiffington was in, more and more faces began to turn her way, their eyes lighting up with interest and recognition as they woke up from the twisted Woleb magic.

"Fetch me my clothes at once," ordered Mayor Noying. "We must get back up there!"

"Fetch your own clothes," snapped Mrs. Noying, the mayor's wife, stepping out of the crowd.

"Oh yes, of course, my dear," the mayor bumbled.

Lucy smiled. The Woleb's powers were fading. The grown-ups were growing up! Not only that, Creakerland was fading too. As Lucy watched, all the roller coasters and wonderfully delicious smells transformed into what they really were, as if a strange mist was lifting. Suddenly she was surrounded by hideous piles of junk and garbage pumping rotten smells into the thick, pungent air.

A second later the ground started to wobble. Lucy had felt this wobble before, when the spider on the map moved its crooked legs.

"The Woleb is moving!" Lucy cried. And she was right! A huge tunnel twisted open in the gnarled walls next to where Lucy and the grown-ups of Whiffington had gathered, and Lucy glimpsed a row of small gleaming eyes looking at her from the darkness.

"What's going on?!" Mrs. Dungston cried.

"It's *them*!" Lucy said, pointing at the eyes.

LUCY IN CREAKERLAND

"Who?"

"The things that snatched you and brought you down here," Lucy said. **"It's the Creakers!"**

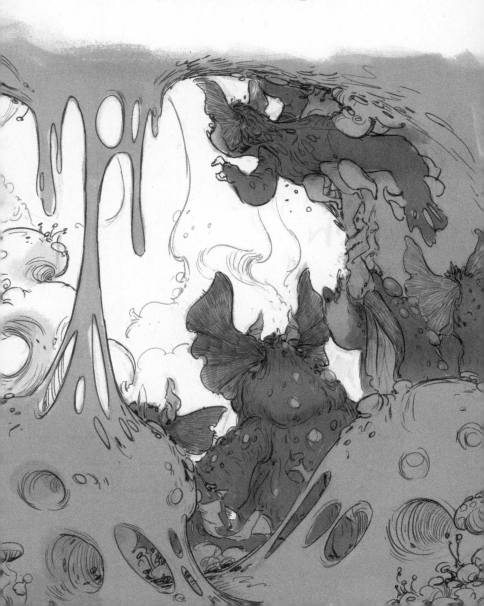

How are you getting on? Sorry I've not spoken to you for a while—I've been busy writing this story, and I guessed you'd be busy reading it. It's all getting a bit topsy-turvy, isn't it? All this upside-down, backward stuff! In fact, if you turn this book upside down and read this page backward, it tells a nice story about fluffy kittens.

... *Only joking. Just wanted to see if you'd turn the book upside down.*

CHAPTER TWENTY-TWO
TRAPPED!

Grunt, Guff, Scratch, and Sniff leapt out of the hole, followed by ten—no, twenty . . . wait, fifty . . . OK, hundreds! Hundreds of slimy Creakers erupted into Main Street, Creakerland, grimacing at the grown-ups as they circled them intimidatingly.

TRAPPED!

"So, the trick's up, innit?" Grunt hissed.

"The humans be seein' the Woleb for whats the Woleb really is," Guff said, flicking his chubby, pointy tail.

The grown-ups backed away, terrified of these hideous monsters, for it was the first time they had seen the Creakers.

"Let us go!" demanded Mayor Noying.

The Creakers burst into what Lucy recognized as Creaker laughter. That very moment, enormous rotten roots burst out of the soggy ground around Lucy and the grown-ups and shot up into the air, where they twined tightly together. They formed a giant cage around the grown-ups, with Lucy hiding somewhere in the middle of the crowd.

We're trapped, she thought.

"Now, where's the kidderling?" Grunt hissed, and Lucy's heart sank as she realized that he was no longer wearing her dad's old coat.

He must have delivered it to the Creaker King, she thought.

"Stay out of sight, Lucypops," whispered Mrs. Dungston to Lucy, pulling her close. But as soon as the words left her mom's lips, Lucy felt the muddy roots

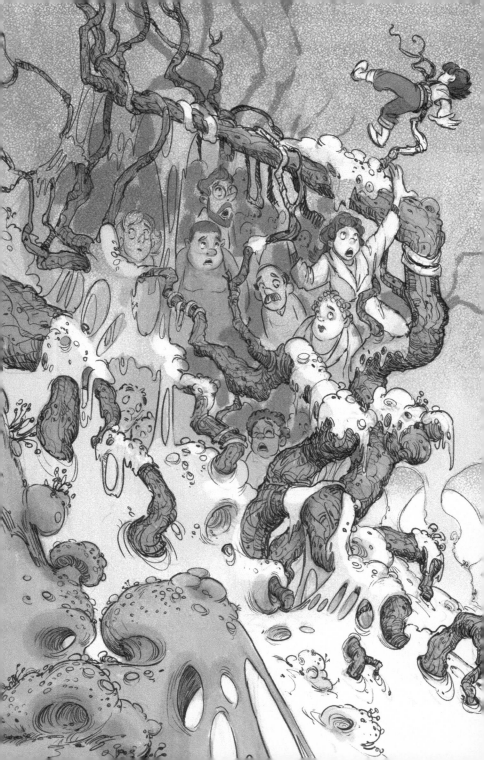

beneath her feet start to rise. They lifted her up into the air, above the grown-ups around her, trying to reveal where she was hiding.

"No, Lucy!" a few of the grown-ups whispered as they fought to hold her down, to keep her hidden.

"Wait!" Lucy said, her mind racing like an engine. "I know what to do. This is the Woleb's power—it's *backward*!" She took a deep breath and yelled at the top of her voice, "I'm right here, look! Easy to see, clear as crystal!"

"Lucy, what are you doing?" Mrs. Dungston gasped in horror.

"It's OK, Mom! Look!" said Lucy, pointing to the Creakers. They were all looking angrily in Lucy's direction—but thanks to Lucy using the Woleb's magic, they couldn't see her at all.

"I think I'd like to stay right here," Lucy announced loudly, and just as she'd hoped, the roots dropped her back down among the crowd.

"You have to do the opposite of what you really want!" explained Lucy to the puzzled grown-ups. "Go backward to go forward, go down to go up. Hide and you'll be seen. Try to be seen and you'll stay hidden! Over here, come and get me!"

The Creakers growled with frustration as they realized they were being outsmarted.

"Tricksy kidderling," Grunt hissed.

"We be comin' backs for your little human!" scoffed Guff.

"We be comin' backs with . . . ," began Scratch.

". . . the king!" croaked Sniff.

"The king knows whats to do with pesky kidderlings," snorted Grunt.

Lucy's heart leapt like a frog as the Creakers disappeared back down the tunnel to summon their leader. She didn't want to be around when they came back.

Once the last Creaker had vanished into the Woleb, all the grown-ups turned to look at Lucy. Dozens of worried, desperate faces stared at her.

"What do the Creakers want from us, Lucy?" asked the mayor, who had managed to find his pajamas and was hurriedly pulling them on.

"Mess!" Lucy said.

TRAPPED!

The grown-ups screwed up their faces in confusion.

"Rubbish!" Piers Snoregan barked.

"Yes, exactly!" Lucy said. "Rubbish! They love our trash, our litter, our mess, muck, mold, and more. They want our waste, and they're tired of all you grown-ups wasting it!"

"Wasting it?" said the mayor, frowning. "But we just throw it away. It's *waste*!"

"Precisely! Then where does it go? Into the oceans? Buried in the ground? Burned up into smoke in the sky?" Lucy said. "These Creakers can't get it if we do that, and without it they can't survive. That's why they snatched you grown-ups and left us kidderlings—I mean, us kids! We're messy and we never clean stuff up. We leave it all out where they can get their hands on it."

"And what were they doing with us down here? What is this place?" shouted Mrs. McScroodles, the candy lady.

"Well, you were all swept away with the power of this world. It makes everything that *is* into *isn'ts,* everything that *was* into *wasn'ts.* Your stressful, grown-up, tidy, mess-free lives became fun and childish again. You were making messes for the Creakers," Lucy said.

"Like cows on a farm," Old Man Carvey said, shaking his head.

"I guess you could say that, yes. A mess farm!" Lucy said.

"Aren't we all forgetting the most important question? How do we get out?" Piers Snoregan asked.

"**SHHHHHHH!**" Lucy said. "If you want something down here, you have to ask in the right way!"

"You mean the wrong way!" Old Man Carvey said.

"Exactly!" replied Lucy, pleased. "A way that this place understands!"

Lucy paced up and down, trying to come up with a plan to get out, trying to think like a grown-up—but her mind was blank. Then she stopped on the spot and rolled her eyes at herself. *Come on, Lucy,* she thought. *Trying to do something in the Woleb is the one sure way of making sure you can't do it!*

She took a new approach. She stopped trying to be the hero who saves all the grown-ups and gets them home safely to their kids. She closed her eyes and cleared her mind. She imagined she was just an eleven-year-old girl who didn't have a clue how to get out of the trap she was in and wasn't really bothered about thinking of a way to rescue all the grown-ups from life on this mess farm.

Suddenly a very clever idea floated through the air and slipped inside Lucy's mind. She felt like a lightbulb had just gone **PING!** above her head, like one of those big red "recording" lights at television studios when they're live on air.

THAT'S IT! thought Lucy. *I mean . . . that's definitely NOT it.*

"Mr. Snoregan!" she said to Piers.

"What?"

"Your television camera. Will it broadcast from down here up to our world?" Lucy said hopefully.

"Certainly not! Heaven knows how deep underground we are. The chances of broadcasting a live television signal out of here are absolutely hopeless!" Piers said.

A huge smile appeared on Lucy's face.

"Perfect—I mean, *Oh no! That's not what I wanted to hear at all!*" she said, winking.

Suddenly the red recording light on top of the *Wakey-Wakey, Whiffington* camera *ping*ed on.

They were live!

Piers Snoregan stared at the camera and scratched his head. "I don't understand it! How did—"

"Never mind that now!" hissed Lucy. "Just pretend you're presenting a normal show."

"Yes, go on! Listen to Lucy!" urged the mayor, nudging Piers toward the camera.

Obediently Piers switched into cheesy-TV-presenter mode.

"Good morning, Whiffington. This is . . ."

"Lucy Dungston!" Lucy interrupted, standing directly

in front of the camera and waving. "Remember me? I'm the girl who wanted to watch the news and go to school . . . and helped you get your hands out of the cookie jars, used the vacuum to suck the Play-Doh out of your noses, and stopped you from crashing all the cars. Well, now I need *your* help!"

She took a deep breath and crossed her fingers for luck. "I really, really, really hope someone is watching this," she said. "This is breaking news! I have found the grown-ups . . ."

CHAPTER TWENTY-THREE
LUCY'S ORDERS

"**W**ould you please be quiet!" Norman grumbled at Ella, who was jumping up and down and yelling in excitement at seeing Lucy on the TV.

"Lucy's there, Norm! She's on the news! I told you so, I told you so!" she sang, dancing in circles.

"Yes, but we have to listen to what she's saying!" He grabbed the remote control and turned up the volume.

". . . I have found the grown-ups," announced Lucy, "and I need your help getting them back."

Ella and Norman gasped.

"Quickly, where's that megaphone?" said Norman, searching the room and then running into the kitchen to keep looking. Triumphantly, he pulled the megaphone Lucy had confiscated out of the fridge.

He ran into the street, placed the now-freezing-cold megaphone to his mouth, and pressed the button.

"CHILDREN OF WHIFFINGTON!" His voice echoed around the houses as little heads poked out of windows and over fences. "LUCY IS ON TV! OUR PARENTS HAVE BEEN FOUND!"

There was a slight pause. Then a tremendous clatter arose in Clutter Avenue as every child stampeded to Lucy's house.

They burst through her front door and gathered in front of her TV set to hear Lucy's announcement together.

"It's Mama and Papa!" Ella cried as Norman came running back into Lucy's living room, squeezing past the crowd of children sitting on children that now filled it. "There they are, in the crowd behind Lucy," Ella said, pointing.

Norman recognized them instantly. They wore matching silk pajamas with their initials sewn on the pockets, and Ella's father had an enormous mayor's hat perched on his head.

"And that's my dad!" gasped Norman, spotting his father. He was pretty easy to see too, as he was wearing his full Scout leader uniform and looked like an oversized, bald version of Norman.

One by one, all the children pointed out their moms and dads, grandmas and granddads. They were even excited to see their teachers!

"There's not much time to explain. You're just going to have to trust me, from one kid to another. I need you to do something. Something no child wants to do," Lucy said into the microphone. Her voice rang out of the TV like a beacon of hope, like a true leader about to ask the impossible of her followers.

"OK, so I'll admit it—we've had fun without the grown-ups. We've stayed up late, eaten all the junk food our bodies desired, and even watched movies rated higher than PG. But it's time we faced reality. Look at the town. Look at yourselves." Lucy paused, but the kids of Whiffington didn't need to look. They knew where Lucy was going with this. They knew she was right. "It's a mess. *We're* a mess. It's time to get the grown-ups back."

There was a burst of applause from inside the packed Dungston living room as the children suddenly realized how much they missed their grown-ups. How much they needed them.

"Here's how we're going to do it," Lucy said. "I need you to do something. You won't enjoy it, but it has to be done. The time has come when we must do our duty and put the needs of these poor, useless grown-ups before our own."

Lucy took a breath, hoping that someone was watching. She had no idea that she had the children of Whiffington hanging on her every word.

"There comes a time when we must . . . **MAKE OUR BEDS!**"

A gasp of horror echoed down Clutter Avenue. The children burst into panicked cries of outrage.

"She's gone doolally," Ella said, twisting her fingers around her head.

"Shhhh!" Norman hissed. "Keep listening!"

"I know it'll be hard. But don't do it for yourselves. Do it for your moms and dads." Lucy stepped out of the way and allowed the camera to film the scared, tired, disheveled-looking grown-ups who were shivering from sugar withdrawal. Off-camera, she kept speaking. "It is time to strip those bedsheets, flip those mattresses, open your curtains and let the sun shine where it never usually shines . . . **UNDER YOUR BEDS!** Children, to your rooms!" Lucy ordered, and at her command the children of Whiffington began marching back to their houses and up to their bedrooms with purpose.

"Right, you heard her!" Norman said as he and Ella scrambled back upstairs and burst into Lucy's bedroom.

"NormEllaTron, assemble!" he boomed.

"What?"

"Er, never mind. Quickly, take off the pillows," he said as he pulled back the duvet and ripped off the sheets. "And open the curtains," he added.

"The curtains? Why?"

"Lucy said to let the sun shine where it never usually shines—under the bed—and that's exactly what we're going to do."

Norman lifted up the mattress and rested it against the wall as Ella pulled the curtains back, allowing the morning sunlight to flood the room with its warmth.

They both stood side by side, staring through the bed slats at the floorboards beneath. Floorboards that were usually kept in darkness, hidden in shadow. Now they were exposed to the sunlight.

All at once Norman and Ella could see what they were hiding. The solid wooden floor beneath the bed bubbled and hissed like a witch's cauldron as the sunlight shone directly on it.

"Norman, look!" Ella said, noticing something out of the window.

From Lucy's bedroom they could see curtains opening in the bedrooms of every house across Whiffington. And as sunlight flooded in through the windows, a strange crumbling sound started coming from the floor. They both jumped back from the unmade bed and saw the strangest thing ever. The floorboards began to shift and wobble, and then they started swirling. What had once been solid wood was now a twirling whirlpool into another world.

"Do you think this is happening in all the other bedrooms in Whiffington?" asked Ella.

"I don't know. But I do know we're going to need some help," Norman said.

"Help with what?"

"This is a rescue mission now, and we're the only ones who know about the Creakers. It's me and you in charge," he said.

"NormEllaTron?" Ella asked.

"Exactly." Norman nodded.

Ella peered into the swirling hole opening up in the floor as the bright morning sunlight filled the room. "Norm, what *is* that?" she asked, putting her pink heart-shaped sunglasses on.

Norman took a deep breath and straightened out his neckerchief. "*That*, my dear Ella, is the way to the Woleb."

CHAPTER TWENTY-FOUR
SUNLIGHT

The red light flickered out. Lucy's broadcast was over.

"Well done, Lucypops," Lucy's mom said, pulling her into a hug.

"Not bad, kid," said Piers Snoregan, "but never interrupt me again."

"Now what?" Mayor Noying whined. *He sounds a lot like his daughter,* Lucy thought.

"Now we wait . . . ," she said.

"For what?"

Lucy grinned. "For *that!*"

She pointed at the large tunnel she'd crept down earlier—the one that led from below Whiffington to

249

Creakerland. Far in the distance, dirt and mud were falling—but not falling *down*, like you would expect. It was all falling **UP!** It was crumbling from the floor all the way up to the ceiling as the

BOOM! BOOM! BOOM

of marching children could be heard echoing through the twisted tunnels of the Woleb from their bedrooms above.

Suddenly a streak of blinding-hot sunlight pierced through the tunnel floor like a laser beam. Everyone jumped and gasped. Mayor Noying let out a high-pitched scream and hid behind Mrs. Noying.

"What in the world is that?" cried Mrs. Dungston.

Lucy smiled. "Sunlight!"

Then another beam of glorious light exploded through one of the wormholes and into the Woleb. Then another, and another, until the entire tunnel was flooded with the most brilliantly warm, fresh morning sunlight.

The walls of the rotten tunnel began melting, dripping like a runny nose, and as the morning sun rose higher in

the sky over Whiffington, its light shone deeper into the tunnel of the Woleb until it finally hit the rotten roots that were trapping the grown-ups and Lucy.

One by one the moldy green bars dried up and turned into powdery dust, crumbling at the slightest human touch into puffs of decayed Woleb powder.

"It's working!" cried Old Man Carvey. "We're free!"

"Not so fast, you rotten stinkers!" screeched Grunt as he and his army of Creakers leapt back into Main Street, Creakerland.

"Arghhh! It be daylight!" Guff cried, seeing the warm light glistening magically out of Whiffington and up into their world, crumbling away the walls of the Woleb.

"She be lettin' in the bright down here," gasped Scratch in horror.

"The kidderling be tryin' to kill us Creakers!" Sniff shrieked as they ducked for cover, hiding themselves in whatever dark shadows they could find. All the other Creakers ran for it, disappearing back down the

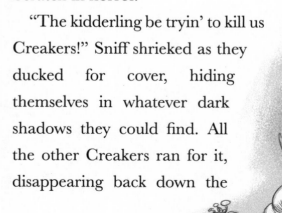

tunnel as fast as they could with stinking smoke billowing from their slimy bottoms as the sunlight touched them.

"Let's go!" Lucy cried, leading all the grown-ups down the tunnel, feeling the kind glow of sunlight on her skin as they arrived at the hundreds of wormholes that led back to Whiffington.

She stood over the first, which was now five times bigger than before and still growing as the sunlight melted away all the rottenness of the Woleb. She shielded her eyes from the light so she could see into it. Once her pupils had adjusted, she saw fifty or so

friendly children peering down at them from her bedroom above.

"NORMAN!" Lucy called, her heart skipping when she saw the unmistakable silhouette of Norman in his Scout uniform.

Lucy could see that he had propped her mattress up against the wall of her bedroom, allowing the fresh sunlight to chase away the shadows beneath her bed, where light never normally reached.

The pure sunbeams were too strong for the rottenness of the Woleb, and with the mattresses out of the way there was no stopping it from penetrating the entrances to the Woleb hiding under every child's bed.

Lucy's plan was working! Or, in Woleb terms, *it was all going horribly wrong.*

"Lucy! Sorry we fell asleep!" Norman shouted back. "But then we saw you on the TV, and we did what you said. We started stripping the bed, and this hole just melted into the floor!"

"Great!" Lucy called. "Well done!"

"I helped too!" called Ella. "We both did. We're NormEllaTron!"

SUNLIGHT

Lucy blinked. "What?"

"NormEllaTron!" Ella shouted back. "Oh—never mind. The stupid name was his idea anyway."

"We're here to rescue you. I hope there's a badge for this!" Norman said. Suddenly a long rope rose up out of the hole in front of Lucy like a snake from a basket. It had perfect knots at regular intervals, ready to be climbed.

As Lucy watched, the Whiffington kids threw ropes into the Woleb through every sunny hole in the squashy floor. There were hundreds of them!

"Norman! These are some of the best knots I've ever seen. I'm so proud of you!" shouted Norman's dad, a tear twinkling in his eye as he gazed at the ropes.

"Thanks, Norman!" Lucy called down into the world above, and Norman gave her a huge smile back.

"Right, grown-ups," Lucy said, looking around. "Take your time climbing out of the Woleb. There's no need to rush."

The grown-ups looked confused for a moment, before Mrs. Dungston caught Lucy's wink and understood. "She's speaking the Woleb's language!" Mrs. Dungston hissed to the grown-ups standing next to her. "Pass it on! What she actually means is . . ."

"HURRY UP! THIS PLACE IS GOING TO COLLAPSE!!!!!" whispered Mr. Quirk.

The grown-ups started climbing down into the holes and back to Whiffington at once. Lucy marched around, overseeing the escape, making sure they all got in. Old Man Carvey, Ella's parents, Paige Turner, and every single mom and dad and grandma and granddad and aunt and uncle of every single boy and girl.

She wasn't leaving anyone behind.

Suddenly the ground shook violently, and more beams of brilliant sunlight exploded sideways out of the wall.

"Lucy, what's happening?" shouted Norman, peering into the Woleb.

"I don't know!" she called. "I think—I think maybe the Woleb is becoming unstable! I don't know how much longer it's going to hold!"

As she said this, a little voice in her mind added, *Or what's going to happen to it once we've all climbed out.*

She glanced back along the winding tunnel and saw the pointy ears of the four Creakers poking out from behind lumps of melting mud and crumbling rock as they hid from the sunlight.

Lucy's heart suddenly sank.

The Woleb is their home, she thought.

Was she really going to leave and let this place turn to dust? Could she really destroy these creatures and their entire world? Lucy didn't want anyone to get hurt—not even the rotten Creakers.

"Lucy, you go first, darling!" Mrs. Dungston said, giving Lucy a little nudge toward the rope.

"No, Mom! YOU go first. I'm rescuing *you*, remember!" Lucy said, and pointed at the rope.

"Oh yes," Mrs. Dungston said, and quickly began

climbing into what was now an enormous hole leading to Lucy's bedroom in Whiffington.

Lucy watched as her mom climbed out and was lifted to safety by Norman.

She had done it!

She was the last human left in the Woleb.

She reached out and grabbed hold of the knotted rope, ready to leave this place behind once and for all. But just as her fist tightened around the rope, she felt someone else's fist tighten about her leg, and she was jerked back into the Woleb.

"AHHHHH!" Lucy screamed.

But how could a Creaker be grabbing her leg? The beams of sunlight pouring up through the holes into the Woleb would surely have turned any normal Creaker to Dozy Dust!

Lucy looked back and got her answer immediately.

This was no ordinary Creaker.

"It's the Creaker King!" Lucy breathed.

Here we go. I told you this was going to happen. I warned you that Lucy would have to face the king. Don't blame me. It's not like I'm making this stuff up. If you didn't go to the bathroom the last time I warned you, then now's your last chance. No? You sure? Because by reading on, you agree to the terms and conditions that I, Tom Fletcher, the author of this book, am not responsible if you pee your pants with fright in the next chapter.

CHAPTER TWENTY-FIVE
THE CREAKER KING

L ucy's stomach twisted in horror as she saw a flash of fluorescent green. She recognized it at once. It was her dad's jacket—and it was draped around the shoulders of the largest Creaker she'd ever seen. He was the size of Guff, Grunt, Scratch, and Sniff put together, a hideously rotten creature who kept himself hidden in the shadows of the tunnel.

With the sun in her eyes from the world above, Lucy could just make out glimpses of the king's cracked lips, his beaky nose, and his flaky, scaly head. His battered, crablike claw was as tough as bone as it grasped Lucy's ankle, but worst of all was his smell. It was like fish guts and vomit. It made Lucy gag.

"Say farewell to your world, kidderling," the king snapped in an awful creaky croak that scratched Lucy's eardrums. He pulled her from the open wormhole, out of the sunlight and back into the dark shadows of the Woleb.

"Get backs from the holes, you disgustin' bunch of twitnits," the king spat at his Creakers. "Or you'll all be dusted!"

Lucy saw the upside-down world turn upside down as he picked her up by the leg with one mighty claw. She was carried, swinging dizzily from side to side, back into the cavernous opening where the entrance to Creakerland had once stood. *Stay calm, Lucy!* she told herself, trying desperately to ignore the leaping of her heart in her chest. *Stay calm!*

With a thud, Lucy was dumped in the middle of Main Street, which was thick, oozing mud now that the polished green pavement had vanished. She rubbed her sore ankle where the king's claw had gripped her as he stood at the entrance to his grand castle

of dustbins. With a wave of his powerful arms, he commanded the brightly lit tunnel that led to Whiffington to twist shut, sealing off the warm sunlight.

"Let me go home!" Lucy shouted at the king, her voice echoing around the enormous cave.

The Creaker King stood very still. Lucy saw his shoulders rise and fall as his rotten, reeking breath filled the air with stinking steam. He reminded Lucy of a fearsome dragon.

He opened his fist, revealing long, black, pointy claws. Lucy gulped.

The king twisted them around, and a huge, greasy throne of mud began to grow out of the floor, bubbling and oozing as it formed in the deepest shadows of the Creaker Castle.

The king suddenly bent forward and creaked along on all fours, more like the Creakers Lucy was used to seeing, although his creak was more creepy, more powerful, like that of a strong silverback gorilla. He crept into the shadows and sat on his moldy throne of rot. If it weren't for the luminous green jacket he'd stolen from Lucy, she wouldn't have been able to see him at all.

"So, kidderling. You've come to destroy us?" The king's voice cut through the darkness.

"No!" Lucy said honestly. "That's not why I came here at all!"

The king was silent for a moment as his four loyal Creakers—Grunt, Guff, Scratch, and Sniff—crept beside his throne.

"These Creakers of mine be tellin' me how you tricksed 'em. How you caught 'em in a sun trap. And now you brings the day down here with yous?" the king said.

"Yes, but I—"

"So, you see, it seems that you are destroyin' us whether you wants to or not."

Lucy's heart sank in her chest. She'd never meant to destroy anything or hurt anyone.

"I just wanted my mom back and to rescue the other moms and dads for the other children," she explained.

"LIES!" the king roared.

Lucy found herself trembling with fear. She wished she could run away, but something about the king made her feel frozen to the spot.

"No kidderling wants their grown-ups back. We takes 'em away—we lets the kids be free, be messy, be naughty," the king boomed. "In return, all we wants is your rotten waste."

"Yes, but . . ." Lucy gulped. "Your Rottenness, you see, it all got a bit out of hand."

"Outs of hand?" the king asked.

"Yes! We realized that we needed the grown-ups. We missed them . . ."

THE CREAKER KING

"*Missed* them?"

"Yes! When they were gone, it was fun for a little while, but then we got lonely and sad. We wanted our moms and dads back." Lucy paused for a moment. "My mom . . . She's all I've got in the world since my dad disappeared. I had to come and save her."

The king was silent. Lucy could only see his large pointy claws dangling over the arms of his throne like spiders sitting on their webs, waiting to attack.

Suddenly the lumpy ground of Main Street started rumbling and shaking. Lumps of decaying floor crumbled upward, floating toward the cave ceiling.

"Your Creakiness," Grunt said in a panic, "the bright be comin' through!"

Lucy knew that Grunt was right. The moldy ground beneath was getting warmer and warmer. As she looked down, a crack appeared by her feet.

"You've got to hide!" Lucy yelled at the Creakers. "Get into the shadows!"

The king stood up, spreading out the long, filthy jacket. Grunt, Guff, Scratch, and Sniff leapt behind it, taking cover in the shadow of their king.

Then the crack split open, and an enormous shard of blinding white sunlight exploded into the cave, slicing through the shadows and falling directly on the king. With a roar, he shielded his face with his arms, protecting it from the hot rays.

"No!" Lucy cried out, terrified they would all be turned to dust.

But the king stood in the pool of light and slowly lowered his arm, allowing the warmth to touch his face.

For the first time Lucy saw what he looked like.

She saw his eyes, which were a twinkling blue.

His nose, which was a little bit big, just like hers.

His mouth, which looked like it might break into a smile at any moment.

A lump instantly caught in her throat, tears formed in her eyes, and her head spun with confusion.

"Dad?!" she gasped, before everything went black.

Chapter Twenty-Six
THE WEIRD WORK OF THE WOLEB

Lucy opened her eyes. Her head swam dizzily, and her stomach was filled with an awful kind of emptiness. She was staring right into a pair of curious, beady black eyes, which blinked at her and then looked up.

"The kidderling be alive, Your Rottenness!" announced Sniff.

The king! Lucy's heart leapt as she remembered what had happened before she blacked out. She rolled slowly onto her side and sat up, wincing.

"Dad?" she called out again, her voice wobbly with worry.

The Creaker King stepped forward from his throne. Grunt, Guff, and Scratch were still hiding in the shadows behind his back, in fear of another beam of light breaking through.

"Whys you be callin' me that, kidderling?" the king said suspiciously.

Lucy nervously took a step toward him so she could see him better. Her knees trembled.

There he was, as clear as crystal.

It was her dad all right, just . . . different.

Changed.

Creakified.

Lucy studied this new face of his.

His ears were long and pointy, like a goblin's, and his skin had turned a dark, wrinkly green. His head was bald—although it had been bald before, so that wasn't any different, but now it was covered in big lumpy moles. His nose was pointy, with twisty, wiry hairs poking out, and in his ears she could see dirty globules of brown wax, like he hadn't washed in years.

But beneath all that, all the rottenness, Lucy knew it was her dad. His eyes still twinkled like magic, and on his left cheek there was a deep dimple, giving him away.

"Dad! What's happened to you?" Lucy whispered in shock, and took another step toward him, reaching out with her shaking hands.

But the king backed away into the shadows. "That's close enough! Is this another tricksy, kidderling?" he demanded fiercely.

"No! Dad, it's me . . . Lucy!"

"Who?"

"Your . . . your daughter . . . Don't you remember?" Lucy said, tears beginning to stream down her cheeks.

"Dad . . . you *have* to try to remember. You're not a Creaker! At least, you haven't always been one. You're a grown-up! With a wife and a kidderling . . . I mean, *kid* . . . ME! Lucy. Your Lucypops . . . remember?"

"Lucypops?" the king repeated slowly, as though he remembered saying that word before.

"YES!" Lucy cried. "That's what you and Mom always call me!"

She saw the Creakers shooting quick, nervous glances at each other.

"The kidderling be tricksin' you, Your Rottenness!" Grunt hissed.

"Best not listen to the tricksy thing," added Guff.

"It's NOT a trick!" said Lucy. "Dad, you disappeared months ago. You just vanished. Everyone thought you'd left us, but I knew you wouldn't do that. Now I know what really happened."

The Creakers all started fidgeting nervously.

"You were snatched!" Lucy's voice echoed around the cavernous room.

"Me? Snatched?" the king scoffed.

"Yes, Dad! By these four rotten things." Lucy pointed

at Grunt, Guff, Scratch, and Sniff. "They snatched you and brought you down here. Who better to be their king than you? The one man who knows garbage better than anyone!"

Lucy stared at her dad's new Creaker face. "You've been here so long, Dad, that this place has changed you. Made you forget. It's turned you all backward and different. But, Dad, I can see you're still in there."

Suddenly another crack burst open in the floor, and a second streak of light shot out into the cave.

"LUCY!" Norman's voice soared up through the hole.

Lucy stared down it. She could see into her world, and Norman waiting for her at the other end.

"Dad, come back with me," Lucy pleaded.

"No, Your Rottenness! This all be a tricks!" Grunt said from his hiding place in the king's shadow.

"It's not a trick, Dad!" yelled Lucy, searching her brain for a way to make her dad remember. She stared at him, standing there in his dirty green work jacket. Then she suddenly remembered . . .

"Dad, your coat pocket!" she exclaimed. "There's something in there. It's yours—remember?"

Slowly the king slid his long black Creaker claw into the coat pocket and pulled out something small, shiny, and silver.

His harmonica!

"You used to play it for me every night," Lucy said hopefully. She gazed at the king's face, watching for any sign that he recognized the object. He held it out in the palm of his hand, staring at it, studying it.

"Trick! Trick! Trick! Trick!" the four naughty Creakers chanted in the king's ear as he turned the silver harmonica around and saw his wretched reflection in its shiny surface.

"What is this thing? This be too shiny and nice to be the Creaker King's," he snapped. "You be tricksin' me, little kidder. I never seen this before."

"NO!" Lucy cried out as he tossed the harmonica through the air. It landed with a splash in what was once the flowing pink milkshake river but was now a stream of moldy, bubbling sludge. Lucy ran to the edge of the stream, but it was too late. The harmonica was gone, sinking deep into the muck, along with all hope of freeing her dad from this Creaker spell.

The Woleb shook violently again, causing huge chunks of mold and festering rot to break away and crumble to dust.

"Lucy, it's *really* time to get out of there!" Norman yelled through the hole from Whiffington, but Lucy didn't budge.

"I can't leave you behind. I won't lose you again, Dad," Lucy said through teary eyes. Her vision must have been blurred, because for a moment she thought she saw a little green teardrop trickle down Sniff's cheek too.

THE WEIRD WORK OF THE WOLEB

As the Woleb collapsed around them, Grunt, Guff, Scratch, and Sniff leapt for cover, shielding themselves from the falling debris anywhere they could. Grunt and Scratch scuffled behind boulders, and a panicking Guff tried to bury himself in the mud. Sniff even dived headfirst into the moldy river.

"Look what you humans have done to our world. To our home," the Creaker King said, looking at his glorious rotten castle, which was beginning to tumble down, one silver garbage can at a time. "We Creakers never wanted to—"

But Lucy had stopped listening. Something had caught her eye. Something impossible.

Something small, shiny, and silver.

"Dad's harmonica!" she whispered as she watched it rise out of the flowing river as though some sort of spell was bringing it back from the dead. Then she saw three black claws clasped around it, and then a bony  arm emerging from the muck. Finally Sniff's head appeared, and the Creaker pulled himself silently out onto the bank of the river, soggy and damp and covered with slime.

"Sniff!" Lucy gasped.

The little Creaker put one claw on his cracked lips and shook his head.

Lucy glanced over to the pile of rubble and mud where Grunt, Guff,and Scratch were hiding. They were staring suspiciously at Sniff.

Scratch spotted the harmonica.

Scratch pointed it out to Guff.

Guff pointed it out to Grunt.

Grunt's eyes narrowed in anger.

But just as he was about to alert the king, Sniff plunged his claw into the black pouch around his neck and blew a clawful of golden Dozy Dust into the air.

The sleepy cloud of dust didn't float lazily this time. It shot like an arrow across the Woleb toward Grunt, Guff, and Scratch.

THUD! FLUMP!
THUMP!

The three Creakers fell fast asleep instantly, collapsing on the floor.

". . . and that's why humans can never be trusted!" the king continued, pacing back and forth, avoiding the cracks appearing in the ground around him.

Sniff creaked silently over to Lucy and, with a wet, trembling claw, handed her the harmonica.

"P-p-please help us," he said, his beady black eyes suddenly large and worried, so that he looked like a sad kitten. Lucy saw something in him she'd not seen in the Creakers before. Kindness.

She took the harmonica, closed her eyes, took a deep breath, and started to play.

Beautiful music suddenly filled every corner of the collapsing cave while she tried to remember "Lucy's Lullaby"—the one her dad used to play to her every night.

The king stopped talking. He froze on the spot as though he could do nothing but listen to the music.

As the notes reached the sleeping Creakers' pointy, cabbage-like ears, they began coming around from the Dozy Dust's spell, shaking off the slumber much faster than humans could.

"Don't listen, Your Rottenness!" they cried, scrunching up their faces as though the beautiful sound was hurting them, but the king couldn't help it. He was already caught in the music's magic.

His cracked green lip was trembling.

He was starting to remember.

"You be turned to dust if you go back," Scratch said in a panicked voice.

". . . *back*?" the king whispered, and Grunt shot Scratch an evil look for confirming the truth.

Huge crystal teardrops formed in the corners of the king's eyes and began falling down his cheeks. Not tears of sadness but of happiness. Happy tears, because every note Lucy played brought his human memories back to him.

Music is more than just sound and noise, more than notes and melodies. Music can transport us to different places. Change the way we feel. Bring back people no longer with us. Music cannot be seen or touched—it has to be felt, and as the king felt it, his head was filled with images of Lucy laughing, playing, and smiling. Images of his wife and his home.

These happy tears fell across his rotten skin, leaving a trail behind them. It was as though they were washing away the wicked work of the Woleb, and the disgusting Creaker he had become was melting at their touch.

When Lucy finished playing, she opened her eyes.

"Let's go home, Lucypops," her dad whispered.

CHAPTER TWENTY-SEVEN
GOING HOME

Mr. Larry Dungston was back! While the Creakers watched in dismay, he grasped Lucy's hand, and together they ran back to the tunnel where the bright circles of sunshine were pouring into the Woleb from Whiffington. Several very worried faces were peering at them through the holes— including Norman's.

"Lucy's back!" he yelled as she came into view. "And she's with—wait! Lucy, is that your dad?"

"Yes—the Creakers snatched him!" she yelled back. "Get ready. We're coming!"

Her dad grasped the nearest knotted rope in one hand and lifted up his Lucypops with the other. Then he tried to pull himself along the rope, but he was too weak. The transformation from Creaker King back to plain old garbage collector had sapped all his energy.

"Norman, we're going to need some help!" Lucy called out.

Norman quickly pulled the rope through the hole toward him. Lucy watched as he looped, twisted, knotted, and pulled it like some sort of Texas cowboy, using every Scout knot he knew. He threw it back to them a minute later. It was now a sturdy harness, big and strong enough for them both to slip over their shoulders.

"Hold on tight!" shouted Norman. "Everybody—PULL!"

Lucy and her dad were suddenly hoisted off the ground. They were pulled away from the Woleb, moving through the glowing wormhole into the glorious sunlight of Whiffington as the crumbling rot of this hidden, secret world decayed around them.

Lucy hugged her father tighter than she'd ever hugged anyone before. She pressed her cheek into the awful stink of his work coat, reveling in the warmth that now filled it, no longer having to imagine he was there.

As they moved along the melting wormhole, Lucy stole a glance into the backward world below and felt a heaviness pull down on her heart. In the shadows she saw Grunt, Guff, Scratch, and Sniff huddled together, shaking with fear as they watched their world, their home, their lives, crumble around them.

THE CREAKERS

The sunlight grew more intense and suddenly broke through the other side of Creakerland, burning a hole even deeper into the Woleb. The walls turned to dust and filled the air with a dull brown mist, and as it cleared, Lucy caught a glimpse of the vast Creaker city. It was the one she'd seen on the map at the center of all those spiderlike legs.

Miles below, there were thousands of Creakers crawling around. Young ones, old ones, families, babies, all scurrying for cover, all desperate to avoid the burning sunlight blasting down into their world of waste and mess. Suddenly the memory of Sniff's wide eyes filled Lucy's mind, and she heard his scratchy voice asking for help. Her heart broke for him and for all Creaker-kind below.

"There you are!" Norman said as Lucy came into view, and he pulled her back into the real world, along with the bunch of scruffy-haired, wild-looking children who had helped to heave them up.

"Norman!" cried Lucy, throwing her arms around him and giving him a huge hug. "Thank you! And thank all of you too," she said to the wild kids.

"Now, off you go and find your parents," Norman said, and with that the filthy children bolted for the door.

"Oh, Norman, this is my dad!" explained Lucy. "Dad, this is my friend Norman."

Norman hopped to attention and gave the best Scout salute he could manage.

"At ease, Norman. Nice to meet you. Any friend of Lucy's is a friend of mine," Mr. Dungston said, attempting his own Scout salute. It wasn't technically correct, but Norman let it go . . . this time.

"Thanks," he whispered to Lucy.

"For what?"

"For telling your dad we are friends."

"I wasn't just saying it, Norman. I meant it," Lucy said, giving him a little nudge with her shoulder.

"Erm, Norman, where are we?" she asked, suddenly realizing that she didn't recognize the room they were standing in. It was decorated in every shade of pink, and unless her eyes were playing tricks on her, it had fluffy wallpaper and the biggest four-poster bed she'd ever seen.

"Wait, let me guess," Lucy said. "Ella's house!"

Norman smiled and they both giggled.

"Where is she?"

"Downstairs with Mrs. Noying and the mayor, thanks to you!"

"But how did you know how to find me?" Lucy asked.

"I figured the Woleb must run underneath most of the town, so when you disappeared, I just kept looking under beds—and there you were!" Norman explained, pointing to the huge mattress and pillows leaning up against the wall, revealing the giant hole leading into the Woleb.

Lucy's heart suddenly leapt like a frog.

"Quickly, put it back!" she cried.

"WHAT?!" Norman gasped as Lucy lunged past him and began remaking Ella's enormous pink bed, slamming the mattress back down, covering the Woleb in shadow.

"They'll all die if we let the sunlight keep pouring in like this. We need to cover up all the holes. We have to tell everyone in Whiffington!"

Norman frowned. "What are you talking about? Who'll die?"

"The Creakers!" cried Lucy. "I know you probably think I'm crazy, but we can't just let them be destroyed." With a final heave, she pushed the mattress over the last slice of sunlight.

Norman's mouth gaped open like a goldfish's.

Mr. Dungston snapped his fingers. "I know! If there's one person who can get the Whiffington folk to pay attention, then you're in luck. You're standing in his house!"

Lucy and Norman stared blankly back at Mr. Dungston.

"The mayor of Whiffington!" he said.

"ELLA'S DAD!" Norman and Lucy cried.

The three of them ran out of Ella's fluffy pink room and downstairs as fast as they could.

"Mayor Noying! Mayor Noying!" they called as they burst into the living room.

"I have no idea how it got marshmallows stuck on it. I promise I didn't wear it, Mama," Ella was saying with a perfect smile as she handed her mother a rather tattered-looking wedding dress.

"All that matters is that we're back together!" Mrs.

Noying replied, throwing the dress aside and pulling Ella in for a hug.

"Sorry to interrupt," Lucy said from the doorway. "But we need help. Ella, where's your dad?"

"I'm very sorry, but he's had to leave," Mrs. Noying said calmly.

"Leave? But you've only just gotten back!" blurted Norman.

"He said he had some work to attend to that couldn't wait," Mrs. Noying replied.

Suddenly Lucy heard the rumble of helicopters thundering in the skies outside, growing louder by the second. Not the normal sort of helicopter sound. This was the sound of huge, hefty, heavy helicopters—and lots of them.

They all ran to the window and stared as a great shadow fell over the entire town.

"What the jiggins?" said Mr. Dungston and Lucy at the same time.

"Well, you don't see *that* every day . . ." muttered Mrs. Noying.

A swarm of hundreds of gray military choppers filled

the sky, flying closely together in formation, with the letters *WAF* stenciled on the side.

"Whiffington Air Force!" cried Norman.

The grown-ups were back—and they meant business!

"What is that thing they're carrying, Dad?" asked Lucy, pointing to an enormous circular machine dangling underneath some of the helicopters on long metal wires and swaying this way and that.

"That's a boring machine," Mr. Dungston said.

"Doesn't look very boring. I'd say it looks pretty interesting," replied Norman, gazing at the metallic goliath whizzing over the town.

"No, it's not a boring machine! It's a machine for *boring* holes!" Mr. Dungston explained. "They're used to dig deep tunnels in the ground, like a big drill."

The frog in Lucy's chest leapt again. She and Norman stared at one another.

"Why is a gigantic tunnel-digging machine being flown into Whiffington by the WAF?" Norman gulped.

Lucy already knew the answer.

"They're going to dig a hole into the Woleb and destroy the Creakers!" she cried.

The image of thousands of helpless Creaker families cowering in the sun's rays flashed through her mind, and she clenched her fists tightly. "I need to stop that machine before it's too late."

"What? Why you?" said Norman.

"I was the one who found the Woleb," said Lucy. "I was the one who worked out that sunlight can destroy it. That means that if the Creakers die, it'll be my fault. I have to be the one to end this."

She looked up at her father. "I need to get to those helicopters, Dad."

Mr. Dungston looked back at his daughter, at the fierce determination in her eyes. She seemed to have grown up suddenly, and this time it wasn't anything to do with strange Woleb magic.

"Right you are, Lucypops. Wait just a jiffy!" he said, zipping up his grubby green coat as he disappeared out of Ella's front door.

"Where's he gone?!" Norman squeaked, but after a few seconds his question was answered by the growl of an engine and the deep hoot of a horn. Norman and Lucy sprinted outside, where Mr. Dungston was pulling up in his stinking, spluttering garbage truck.

"Quickly, get in!" he said, leaning over and opening the passenger door.

"In *that* thing?" Norman asked.

"Yeah. That OK?" asked Mr. Dungston.

"AWESOME!" Norman cried, pushing past Lucy to jump in first.

Lucy, Norman, and Mr. Dungston charged through the streets of Whiffington in the Muck-Mobile—that's what Norman had decided to call it—trying to follow the helicopters overhead. They lurched around corners so fast that half the trash in the back spilled out onto the streets, leaving a wake of whiff on every street they sped down.

"Sorry!" Mr. Dungston yelled out of his window. "I'm used to picking up garbage, not dropping it off!"

"Where are they going?" Lucy shouted as they whizzed along.

"Dunno, Lucy! Just don't take your eyes off 'em!"

"There's a slight northwesterly wind, so taking that into account with their approximate heading, I'd say they were going . . ." Norman paused.

"Where, Norman?" cried Lucy.

"But—that can't be right . . . ," he muttered.

"I can't see them anymore!" Mr. Dungston yelled as the helicopters whizzed below a line of tall trees and then disappeared behind the houses of Whiffington, carrying the whopping great drilling machine out of sight.

GOING HOME

"Dad, I've got an idea! Turn left!" Lucy cried.

"But they didn't go le—"

Mr. Dungston didn't get the chance to finish his sentence as Lucy leapt over and yanked the massive steering wheel toward her. The Muck-Mobile skidded round a corner, pulling into—

"Trampoline Avenue!" Lucy exclaimed as she jumped out of the truck and onto the nearest trampoline. "We might be able to spot them!"

Norman and Mr. Dungston followed, the pavement beneath their feet suddenly turning soft and bouncy. They all bounced along it, jumping as high as they could, trying to catch a glimpse of the helicopters and their machine.

"Can—you—see—them?" Lucy yelled with each bounce as their three heads bobbed up and down above the rooftops.

When they came to the end of the street, they were completely exhausted.

"Sorry, Lucy. We lost 'em!" Mr. Dungston said.

"I . . . th-th-think—I . . . ," Norman panted, not able to get his words out.

"What is it, Norman?" Lucy asked.

He took a deep breath and gulped.

"The . . . helicopters . . ."

"Yes?"

"I saw them . . ."

"Where?"

"They were hovering—directly over YOUR HOUSE!" Norman gasped.

"You mean we've been chasing them all this time while they've been flying toward *our* house?" cried Mr. Dungston.

"Of course. It makes perfect sense!" Lucy realized. "Our house was where I discovered the Woleb, and where sunlight first entered its shadowy tunnels. It's the perfect place to drill! It's where everything began."

"It's where everything could end," said Norman.

"I just hope we're not too late!" Mr. Dungston said as they bounced back into the Muck-Mobile and raced toward their home.

The closer they got, the more intense the noise became, like driving into the heart of a thunderstorm. The rumble of the helicopters' rotor blades set off car alarms, and made glass windows rattle and shingles slip off rooftops, smashing to the ground below.

As they pulled onto Clutter Avenue, Lucy saw the most unbelievable thing she'd ever seen—even more unbelievable than the Woleb. Through the dusty windscreen of the Muck-Mobile she could make out at least a hundred WAF helicopters hovering over her little house, circling like a tornado of hungry vultures. Beneath them hung the whopping great drilling machine, swinging around like a metallic shark and baring its teeth at the roof of the Dungston home.

The sight was enough to make Mr. Dungston slam on the brakes, bringing the Muck-Mobile to an abrupt halt.

"How on earth are you ever going to stop *that*, Lucy?" said Norman. "Lucy . . . ?" he repeated, looking around.

But there was no reply.

The passenger door was open, and Lucy's seat was empty.

"Where's Lucy gone?!" Norman cried.

Lucy wasn't wasting any time. She was sprinting as fast as she could toward the chaos, scrambling over car hoods and stumbling through flower beds, until she burst through her front gate and disappeared into the hallway.

"LUCY! WAIT!" Mr. Dungston cried out of the window, honking the horn of the garbage truck before leaping out and racing toward his house. Suddenly dozens of figures in dark uniforms flew down from the sky above and landed with a thud around him: Whiffington Air Force rappelling down from the choppers above. They formed a line across the street, forcing him to stop.

"Sorry, sir. This is off-limits now," the nearest officer said firmly.

"But that's my house! And my daughter is in there!" Mr. Dungston said.

SCREEEEEEECH!

CRASH!

CHOMP!

An ear-shredding sound sliced through the air as the teeth of the gigantic drill pierced the top of Lucy's house. The officers ducked for cover as the chimney was obliterated, sending bricks raining down into the street and punching deep dents in Mr. Dungston's truck.

"GET BACK!" barked the WAF. "This street is now closed!"

And with that, they clapped their hands on Mr. Dungston's shoulders and marched him to the far end of the street, away from the house, away from the choppers, away from Lucy.

She was on her own.

This is it. You're almost there. Only three chapters to go and you'll know how it all ends. I already know what happens. If I wanted to, I could spoil it for you right now by saying that Lucy gets chopped to bits by the big drill and is never seen again. Or perhaps Lucy gets superpowers and melts the drill with laser beams from her eyeballs. Maybe both those would make better endings than what really *happened. There's only one way to find out . . .*

CHAPTER TWENTY-EIGHT
THE WHOPPING GREAT DRILLING MACHINE!

L ucy closed the front door behind her, which rattled on its hinges under the intense vibration. In fact, the entire house was rattling. Can you imagine a hundred helicopters swirling around over your house with a whopping great drilling machine, ready to blast in through your ceiling at any moment?

No, thank you very much! Sounds absolutely awful, doesn't it?

Lucy ran upstairs, leaping up two or three steps at a time.

Faster, Lucy! Faster! she commanded herself.

She burst into her bedroom. Her bed lay like a bridge over the large wormhole leading down to the Woleb, her mattress still leaning against her bedroom wall. She quickly drew the curtains, shutting out the sunlight, and threw her mattress down onto the bed, casting everything underneath it into deep, dark shadows.

The instant the darkness returned, Lucy saw the most incredible thing happen. The hole started swirling and shrinking, like the way water goes down the drain in the bath.

The darkness was healing the damage she had done.

SCREEEEEECH!

CRASH!

CHOMP!

303

Suddenly the whole room started shaking. Lucy wobbled and stumbled to her knees. Her bedside table tipped over, and her books flew off their shelves. Her jelly-bean-eating-competition certificate fell off the wall, and the frame shattered on the floor. Her sock drawer slid open, sending socks flying everywhere! It was mayhem.

Then came the worst sound of all.

It was a sound like she'd never heard before.

And why would she?

It was the sound of the roof being ripped right off her house.

Giant, shiny silver teeth sliced into the Dungstons' roof, drilling right into Lucy's bedroom.

Lucy glanced at the door—but there wasn't time to make a run for it now. The drill was coming down. There was no escape. Below her was the shrinking entrance to the Woleb; above her, the menacing metal teeth of the whopping great drilling machine.

Lucy was caught in the middle. Right between grown-ups and Creakers.

SCREEEEEECH!
CRASH!
CHOMP!

And, just like that, the whole ceiling suddenly came right off.

All the roof shingles, the bricks, her glow-in-the-dark stars: everything went swirling into the shimmering, spinning jaws of the mighty military drill.

Lucy felt sunlight fall on her face, and for a moment she understood what it must feel like to be a Creaker. That heart-stopping dread of your world about to be turned to dust. Although it wasn't the sunlight itself that would be turning Lucy to dust—it was the screeching drill, getting closer and closer every second.

Lucy looked around. The sight before her was so mind-bogglingly weird. Her bedroom had four walls— and NO ceiling. There was just a great big hole overhead, filled only by the approaching Creaker-killing machine and the whirring of helicopter blades.

The drill suddenly dropped lower, eating up the walls of Lucy's room too. The windows smashed. The curtains got sucked into the grinding teeth, and a tornado of bricks turned to rubble as they tumbled down into the yard below.

Lucy was now standing in her bedroom with no ceiling above her and no walls around her. It was just her and her bed, completely open to the outside world.

"LUCYPOPS!" a voice called out over the screaming of the drilling machine, and Lucy caught a glimpse of her father and mother at the end of her street, waving at her desperately. It wasn't just them being held back by the military. Norman was there with his dad. Ella stood with her mama. The whole of Whiffington had gathered in a great crowd. Even the *Wakey-Wakey, Whiffington* cameras were rolling, ready to capture the destruction of the Woleb.

It was at that moment, standing beneath a hundred helicopters with a giant drill a few inches away from her head, being watched by the entire population of Whiffington Town, that Lucy realized something.

Something very weird.

She wasn't scared.

Of course, it was terrifying to have a whopping great drill rip off your roof and dangle a few inches from your head, about to be dropped at any moment right on the spot you're standing in—but somehow Lucy had come to realize that what she was about to do was bigger than being scared. More important than feeling frightened.

She was standing up for what she believed in. Putting the lives of others before her own. Lucy had been prepared to risk everything to save the grown-ups from the Creakers—and now she was risking it all to save the Creakers from the grown-ups.

"STOP!" she shouted.

But the machine kept drilling. Getting lower and lower.

SCREEEEEEECH!

"STOP DRILLING!!!" she called.

CHOMP! CHOMP! CHOMP!

the machine replied.

Lucy realized that screaming was no good. She had to be *seen*. She stood up on her bed, making herself as tall and as big as she possibly could. She raised her open palms toward the drill, and this time she demanded that it obey her.

"THAT'S ENOUGH!" she ordered.

With a great

CLAAAANKKK!
HISS!

and a **PSHHHHHH!** the whopping great drilling machine came to a sudden halt.

Lucy stared up at the sharp metal face of the drill. Its pointy tip was barely an inch from her open hand.

"Raise the drill!" echoed an angry voice through a megaphone from one of the helicopters above.

The choppers' engines roared as they lifted the drill out of the Dungston family's home.

"Well, what is it, Sergeant?" the voice echoed down from above again, and Lucy recognized it now. It was

Mayor Noying—Ella's dad. He was hanging out of the side of one of the great helicopters, peering down with a stern frown across his forehead.

"It's . . . it's the girl, sir!" the nervous sergeant replied.

"A *girl*?"

"No! *THE* girl. The one who rescued us all from the Woleb."

"It's me, Lucy!" Lucy shouted back up at the WAF choppers through the megaphone she'd confiscated. "Lucy Dungston, and this is my home!"

"Well, for goodness' sake, Lucy, get out of the way! We've got to get rid of those disgusting vermin down there," the mayor demanded.

But Lucy didn't get out of the way. She sat down on her bed and folded her arms.

"I'm not going anywhere," she said. "If you want to kill those poor little creatures, you'll have to chomp me up with your drill too."

There was silence. (Well, apart from the sound of all the helicopters, obviously.)

Then a rope suddenly dropped down through Lucy's open ceiling. Lucy looked up to see the mayor whizz down the rope from the chopper, his chunky golden chain and pointy hat flapping in the breeze.

"Now, listen here, little girl," he boomed into his megaphone seconds before he landed, his shiny boots clomping on her bedroom floor.

"No. *YOU* listen," Lucy said into her own megaphone, standing up on her bed so that she was just as tall as the very cross mayor. "I'm not moving from this spot. This is my room. My home. And you've got no right to come flying over here with your big chompy machine and slice off my ceiling."

"But—but—" the mayor stuttered. He'd never been spoken to like this by any child other than Ella before, but that was usually about lumps in her mashed avocado or staying up late.

"No buts," Lucy continued. "This isn't just *my* home. This is *their* home too." She pointed down to the shadows beneath her bed.

"But those *things* snatched us all away! They nearly turned us all into messy, silly children!" the mayor spluttered.

"Yes. And that was wrong of them. But you are as much to blame as they are."

"What?!"

"You heard me!" Lucy's voice blasted out loud and clear for all of Whiffington to hear. "You, me, and every single person here in Whiffington. We're just like those creatures. They have homes. They have families. And they're sick and tired of watching us dump all our trash when they can turn it back into something useful. Our garbage can give a Creaker child a bed. It can build a family a home. It can even power a whole city! If only we could work together instead of trying to snatch or destroy each other. We might look different, and we might not see the world the same way, but that doesn't mean we can't all live on it and under it together. Peacefully. Happily!"

Lucy looked out from her crumbling bedroom to the crowd gathered at the end of her street. They were listening to every word she said—and she saw lots of them nodding.

"But—but this is madness. You can't listen to *her*! She's just a child," the mayor pleaded to Whiffington.

"That's right. I *am* a child. Just a kid. The kid who saw you running NAKED through Creakerland."

The mayor looked out to see Ella and Mrs. Noying standing in the crowd. Ella put her heart-shaped sunglasses on and acted like she didn't know him.

"The kid who brought you all back to your families," Lucy continued. "The kid who knows that if we drill this hole, we'll destroy the Creakers forever."

The mayor said nothing. He was dumbstruck by Lucy's words. Lucy was seeing the world far more clearly than any grown-up had for a very long time.

The mayor bowed his head in shame.

"Lucy, I've been a fool," he sighed, removing his tricorn hat and placing it on Lucy's head. "You have reminded us all that sometimes children can see the truth that grown-ups have forgotten how to see."

He lifted the megaphone to his mouth. "Call off the whopping great drill!" he ordered with a wave of his hand, and the helicopters instantly flew the machine away.

"We've been complete fools, haven't we?" the mayor said to Lucy.

"No, you've just been grown-ups."

"I don't suppose you have any idea what we should do next?" asked the mayor sheepishly. He'd never had to ask anyone what he should do before—especially not a kid.

Lucy looked around at the mess she was standing in. There were no walls, no ceiling, no wardrobes. Just Lucy, the mayor, and her bed.

Lucy smiled.

"What is it?" the mayor asked.

"I think I have an idea."

CHAPTER TWENTY-NINE
LUCY'S BIG IDEA

"OK, only one more house," Lucy said to her dad as she wound down the window of his stinky garbage truck.

They pulled up outside Ella's house.

"Good evening, Mayor Noying," Mr. Dungston said, jumping out of the truck with a chirpy tip of his flat cap.

The mayor came out of his front door, struggling with three heavy bags of trash, while Mrs. Noying and Ella watched from the doorway, giggling quietly.

"Evening, Mr. Dungston. Good evening, Lucy," he said.

"Lovely pajamas!" Lucy said, trying not to burst out laughing at the mayor's neatly ironed pink silk pj's.

"Thank you. Ella got them for me," he mumbled. "Are we all set for tonight?"

"Yes, I think everything's ready," Lucy replied from the passenger seat of the smelly truck.

"Good. We shall see you at sunset, then, young Lucy. Fingers crossed your plan works!" the mayor said.

Mr. Dungston threw the mayor's trash bags into the back of the truck and jumped into the driver's seat.

"See you there!" Lucy called out to Ella, and waved.

They whizzed around Whiffington as the evening sun dropped low in the sky.

"Lucy," Mr. Dungston said. "No matter what happens tonight, I'm proud of you."

"Thanks, Dad," Lucy said. "I just hope it works."

"Me too, Lucypops. Me too."

They stopped off at their home, which was halfway through being repaired from the damage caused by the whopping great drill. Mrs. Dungston stepped out of the front door, edged her way around the scaffolding, and hopped into the truck with them. She was wearing her bathrobe and pj's and looked ready for bed.

"Oh, it feels so good to have you home," she said,

throwing her arms around Mr. Dungston's neck and giving him a big kiss.

"Not as good as it feels to *be* home!" he replied with a huge grin on his face.

"Ready for the big night, Lucypops?" Mrs. Dungston asked.

"I am. I just hope *they* are!" Lucy said with a hint of nervousness in her voice.

They drove through the streets to a place Mr. Dungston knew like the back of his grubby hand. The sign swinging outside the entrance read WHIFFINGTON DUMP.

But tonight it looked rather different.

It was no longer Whiffington Dump. It was *Camp Whiffington.*

As they pulled in through the gates, they were greeted by two familiar faces.

"Hi, Mr. Quirk! Hey, Norman!" Lucy said as she jumped down from the truck. "Is everything going as planned?"

"Indeed it is, Lucy! The campsite is up and running," replied Mr. Quirk.

"No flashlights, right?"

Norman lifted up a huge bag full of confiscated flashlights, and Lucy smiled.

"Everything's under control, Lucy. Scout's honor," Norman said with a salute. "That reminds me—this is for you."

He pulled a green-and-yellow scarf and a little neckerchief slide out of his pocket. He placed the scarf around Lucy's neck, fastened it with the slide, and straightened it.

"Welcome to Whiffington Scout Troop," he told her, smiling.

"Aha! Do we have a new member?" Norman's dad called, popping his Scout leader hat on his head excitedly.

Lucy looked into Norman's hopeful eyes, then around at the wonderful work he and his father had put into Camp Whiffington.

"Actually, it's *two* new members!" Lucy said, noticing that Ella had just arrived. "Hey, Ella!"

"Hi, Lucy. Good evening, Norman," Ella said politely, being a cute little angel now that her mama and papa were back.

"Ella, I've just signed you up for the Whiffington Scout Troop with me."

"You did WHAT?!" Ella whispered in horror.

"That's right. You're a Scout now."

"I certainly am not."

"You are if you don't want your mama to find out that you went skipping through Whiffington in her wedding dress," Lucy whispered.

"Well, this is fantastic news!" Mr. Quirk cried. "New recruits are most welcome. We don't get many, do we, Norman? In such unusual circumstances, I'm delighted to present you both with your first Scout badges." And with that, he whipped out two circular woven patches and handed one to Lucy and one to Ella.

"The *starting-a-new-adventure* badge," he said.

Lucy slicked her hair to one side, looked at the small patch in her hand, and felt her cheeks turn a little red. She couldn't stop the corners of her mouth from turning up with pride. She glanced over at Ella, who was wearing the exact same expression but quickly put her sunglasses on to hide it. They both suddenly knew why Norman took his badges so seriously.

Norman proudly pointed to the same badge sewn on his jumper and gave them both a thumbs-up.

"And may I ask how you both came to hear about the Whiffington Scout Troop?" asked Mr. Quirk.

Ella pointed her finger at Norman accusingly. Lucy nodded in agreement.

"Then, if I'm not mistaken, there is one more badge to be awarded tonight," Mr. Quirk said. "For getting one or more people to join our troop, for bringing people together, Norman . . ."

Norman got down on one knee and looked more like he was being knighted by the queen than being handed a Scout badge by his dad.

". . . I award you the *friendship* badge," said Mr. Quirk, handing over the little patch.

Lucy and Ella applauded as Norman stared at the badge. He let out a big sigh.

"What's wrong?" Lucy asked.

"It's just . . . I've just wanted this badge for so long," Norman muttered, rubbing his thumb over it.

"And now you have it, Norm!" Ella said, nudging him.

"Yeah, I know. But I've just realized it wasn't the *badge* I wanted," Norman said, his cheeks flushing red. "It was the friends that came with it."

Lucy put her arm around his shoulders and gave him a squeeze.

"I think I'm going to be sick," Ella mumbled.

"Lucypops, it's nearly time," Mr. Dungston called.

There was a huge crowd starting to gather in Camp Whiffington. Families were pitching tents and laying blankets on the ground. The smell of hot chocolate boiling over campfires hung in the air as the grown-ups shared stories of their time in the Woleb—while the children kept their own adventures secret.

"Nearly sunset," Lucy heard them whisper.

321

"I wonder if they'll show up," said another.

The crowd parted, allowing Mr. Dungston's smelly vehicle to pull up, with Lucy, Norman, and Ella walking beside it. Mr. Dungston jumped out to join Lucy, and her heart pounded in her chest as something wonderful came into view in front of her.

On the spot where there was once a great big pile of stinking, rotting waste now sat something marvelous. Something genius. Something only a child could think of. A whopping great BED!

It had four thick tree trunks for posts, and as Lucy and her dad got closer, a swarm of Whiffington Air Force

helicopters lowered a monumental mattress the size of a football field, plus a humongous pillow stuffed with hundreds of normal-sized pillows, down into place on top of the bed.

It was the most incredible thing Lucy had ever seen.

Although it was a bed fit for a giant to sleep in, no one would be lying in it. It wasn't made for sleeping in. It was the deep, dark, shadowy patch beneath the giant bed that really mattered.

As Mr. Dungston and Lucy walked up to the enormous bed, the crowd cheered and whooped.

"There she is!"

"That's Lucy!"

Lucy nervously unloaded the last few sacks of garbage and tossed them onto the pile of stinking trash bags, old furniture, and other bits and pieces at the bottom of the bed. She took a step back and admired the mountain of Whiffington's filthy, rotten garbage— the town's peace offering to the Creakers.

Then Lucy, her mom, and her dad found a spot in the crowd, a little distance away from the enormous bed. Mr. Dungston rolled out three sleeping bags, then reached into his pocket and pulled something out.

"Want to try to beat your record, Lucypops?" he said, waving a bag of jelly beans in the air with a smile.

"Impossible!" her mom chuckled.

Lucy and Mr. Dungston gave each other a look, and both said at exactly the same time, "Impossible isn't real!"

And the three of them burst out laughing.

The sun slowly set over Whiffington. Everyone stared longingly into the darkness beneath the enormous bed, looking, hoping, for any sign of movement.

As the night drew on with not the slightest creak, flasks of hot chocolate ran dry, and the sound of tired yawns grew more frequent as the campfires calmed to glowing embers.

"I don't think they're coming," Lucy heard someone whisper.

"It hasn't worked!" said someone else.

"Should we all go home?"

"What do we do now?"

"We wait!" Lucy said. "Give them time!"

But time ticked on, and still there was not even the slightest sign of a Creaker. Lucy stared as hard as she could into the blackness beneath the oversized bed, willing herself to see some sort of movement. But all she saw was the piles and piles of dirty trash, sitting there, stinking out the night.

Was this all just a silly, childish idea? Building a giant bed, collecting the town's garbage in the evening and leaving it out for the Creakers to take?

Please, Grunt, Lucy thought.

Please, Guff, Lucy hoped.

Please, Scratch and Sniff, Lucy wished.

She didn't dare take her eyes off the shadows. She just stared at the blackness. The darkness. The nothing.

Nothing . . .

CHAPTER THIRTY
WAKEY-WAKEY, WHIFFINGTON!

Lucy sat bolt upright. Her mind was racing, her heart pounding. Somehow, while staring at the shadowy nothing, she'd drifted off to sleep.

It was still dark. Stars twinkled overhead as she looked around Camp Whiffington and saw that everyone had done the same. Everyone was peacefully snoozing away.

Old Man Carvey was wrapped up in his fluffy robe. Paige Turner had fallen asleep with her nose in a book.

Mayor Noying was snoring into his megaphone.

All was peaceful.

Lucy sighed as she glanced down at her sleeping parents. Although her plan hadn't worked, she had succeeded in one thing—bringing her parents back. Not just back from the Woleb but back together. She looked at their happy, sleeping faces, and even though their eyes were tightly shut, she knew there was love in them.

But that wasn't all Lucy saw.

She leaned in close for a better look at her mom's and dad's eyes.

Her heart leapt!

In the corners were the unmistakable little crumbly drops of . . . **DOZY DUST!**

She quickly glanced around at everyone else. They all had Dozy Dust in their eyes too!

Slowly she raised her hand up to her own face and wiped the corners of her eyes. As she lowered it, her heart began beating so hard that she was sure it would wake everyone up. There, on the tips of her fingers, were little nuggets of golden Dozy Dust.

She looked toward the whopping great bed, and a huge smile crept across her face.

WAKEY-WAKEY, WHIFFINGTON!

While they were all asleep, the enormous pile of Whiffington garbage had mysteriously disappeared in the night. Just like magic. Just as Lucy had planned.

"It worked!" Lucy whispered to herself, grinning from ear to ear.

Her smile was suddenly greeted by the warmth of the rising sun. It peeked over the tops of the four trees acting as giant bedposts, and began chasing away the shadows.

Lucy glanced around at the townspeople as they lay snoozing, blissfully unaware that her plan had worked; that Lucy, the kid, had found a way for them all to live together in harmony; that despite their differences, it was possible for human and Creaker to coexist.

As the sunlight melted the night, replacing shadows with the warm orange glow of morning, Lucy looked at the last remaining spot of darkness beneath the giant bed—where four pairs of twinkling black eyes quickly disappeared into the world below.

THE END

OK, so that's it. Story over. I hope you enjoyed it. What do you mean, "What happened next?" I've already written THE END. I don't think I'm allowed to write anything else after that. It's the rule.

. . . Oh, all right. Maybe just a little bit.

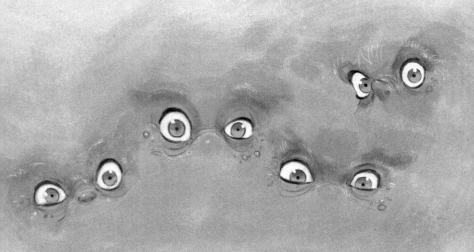

Epilogue
TOMORRA

Grunt, Guff, Scratch, and Sniff creaked back into the Woleb, dragging with them bags and bags of glorious Whiffington trash.

"Looks at all this mucky mess we gots!" cheered Guff.

"More than we've never snatched before!" yelled Scratch.

"And we didn't 'ave to do 'ardly any creakin'!" added Grunt, sounding quite amazed.

"All this 'sgusting garbage, just sittin' there for us to snatch, just likes that!" croaked Guff with rotten delight.

"All thanks to the kidderling!" said Sniff happily.

Grunt stopped suddenly, causing the other Creakers to bump into him. He turned and stared at Sniff, looking deep into his round black eyes. No Creaker had ever said a nice word about a kidderling before. They were so used to hiding from kidderlings in the shadows beneath their beds, sneaking into their rooms, and creaking around their houses. Being *nice* about a kidderling was something new. Something strange.

"His brain must be rotted," laughed Scratch nervously, worried that Grunt was angry at Sniff. "He just needs a good slop at the tavern."

"No . . ." Grunt whispered. "Sniff be right! If it weren't for the kidderling, this place would be all sunburned, and we'd all be dusted. She saved us." He gazed with astonishment at Sniff. "And Sniff saved the girl. That means . . . *Sniff* saved us!"

Sniff kicked the ground with embarrassment, not knowing where to look. Guff and Scratch were stumped.

Things were changing in the Woleb—changing for the better.

"And looks!" went on Grunt. "We's got enuff rotten mess in one night to last us a whole week!" He pointed at the huge pile of smelly prizes they were hauling behind them.

"We's not be needin' to creak up there every night like we used to," agreed Sniff. "We's be able to—"

"Spend more time with our Creakerlings!" Grunt interrupted Sniff, which took Sniff by surprise, as it was usually him that did all the butting-in.

"P'raps kidderlings be not so bads after all," Sniff suggested.

They dragged the heavy load of Whiffington garbage deep down into the depths of the Woleb, clawing out rotten gifts to Creakers they passed on the way.

They gave Mrs. Blister boxes and boxes of broken egg-shells to rebuild the Creaker school that had crumbled to pieces in the Wolebquake. "No thank you!" she cried as she accepted them excitedly.

Sergeant Gurgle and Major Curd, two Woleb police officers, siphoned all the curdled milk to use as fuel for the Woleb police cars.

Claggy Maggot and Maggie Clog, owners of Maggot & Clog's Grossery Store, collected all the banana peels, moldy vegetables, and fish bones to sell in a week or so, once they'd matured a bit.

Eventually Grunt, Guff, Scratch, and Sniff had delivered all the rotten delights to the hardworking Creakers of the Woleb below Whiffington as they rebuilt their weird home. There were boos and hisses as the four Creakers passed through. It was a real heroes' welcome.

Grunt had been deep in thought, his mind turning something over as they creaked through the town. Suddenly he leapt up to the top of a heap of rot and motioned for the crowd that had gathered to quiet down.

"Fellow Creakers!" he bellowed, and the hundreds of slimy creatures hushed and listened. "We be startin' a new time. We be rebuildin' ourselfs a new Woleb." The crowd booed in agreement. Grunt continued. "And this new Woleb needs a new king!"

Silence fell. Grunt stood atop the pile, looking as powerful as a Creaker could look.

"GRUNT FOR KING! GRUNT FOR KING!" the crowd began chanting.

Grunt held up his hand, and silence fell again like magic.

"I would be honored to be your king," he croaked, and the crowd booed in celebration.

"BUT!" added Grunt.

The booing was instantly replaced by confused whispers.

"But I thinks this *new* Woleb needs a king with *new* ideas. A king with a new way of thinkin'," Grunt boomed, staring into the eyes of his fellow Creakers. "Someone who's not 'fraid to be different. To stands up for whats he believes to be right." He turned and suddenly pointed his claw at a Creaker behind him.

"Someone like Sniff!"

Gasps erupted from the crowd as all eyes turned to the small boil-covered Creaker standing in Grunt's shadow.

"Sniff dared to trust the kidderling when no one else did. He dared to be different. It was Sniff what saved you!" cried Grunt as he dropped to his knee and bowed his bald head to Sniff.

There was a pause as hundreds of Creakers stared at this teensy Creaker. Then, one by one, they dropped to their knees and bowed in respect to their new leader. He was the one who had helped to save the Woleb.

Sniff stared out at his disgusting kingdom and let out a little excited squeak.

Grunt announced, "All hail His Rottenness, King—"

"SNIFF!" Sniff blurted out, interrupting Grunt in utter disbelief.

The Creakers had a new king.

"Well, that be it," said Grunt, handing out the final scraps from the bottom of the last trash bag to Guff, Scratch, and King Sniff. "Takes whatever's left home for yer families."

"See you tomorra?" Guff said, his bottom releasing a little parp.

"No, not tomorra. I thinks we's be all right takin' a

little time off from creakin'." Grunt smiled. "That's if the king approves?"

"Oh . . . erm—yeah!" Sniff stuttered, trying to get used to the whole *King of the Creakers* thing.

With that, Grunt gave the three of them a little salute and left them standing in the twisted Woleb tunnel. He creaked all the way along the winding spider leg and didn't stop until he was standing outside a dark crack in the wall of the Woleb, the entrance to his home.

The foul stench of stewing sprouts filled the air, and he took a deep sniff of his wife's awful cooking.

"Home, sour home!" he sighed as he stepped inside and was greeted by the most wonderful sound in all the Woleb.

"Daddy!"

THE END

. . . . again

Creaker-Speak

Dozy Dust
The Creakers' powder that sends you to sleep

Dunglicker
Not a very nice word—don't call your teacher this

Kidderling
A child

Quickybit
Quickly

Sprog
Another word for a child

Stinkerful
Smelly

Twozzle
A really silly person

Twizzle
A silly person

Washy-brained
Confused

Woleb
The world beneath your bed, where Creakers live

ACKNOWLEDGMENTS

My name sits proudly on the front of this book but the truth is, as lovely as that is for my ego, there should be a whole bundle of names splattered across the cover. It's a real team effort, and I would like to thank them by giving them all a weird, awkward cuddle—instead, though, I'm just going to write something nice about them here. . .

First I must start by thanking Shane Devries—your illustrations are the most awesome that I've ever seen, and I'm so honored to have my silly words brought to life by you. Fletch, I hope it goes without saying that none of this would have happened without you. Literally none of it! I'd just be a strange, unsociable blob gathering dust at my piano. Thanks for always dreaming bigger than anyone. David Spearing, if it weren't for our weird late-night whatsapps and you literally saying the words "THE CREAKERS" to me, then this book would never have happened, and I can't thank you enough for all your ideas and directorial wizardry on all the videos we make. Michael Gracey, thanks so much for spending time thinking about sticky monsters under the bed while making *The Greatest Showman*. As always, your ideas were so inspiring and took the Creakers to the next level of disgusting! Stephanie Thwaites, you're a brilliant agent for originally seeing the potential in the poop that I write and believing in me from the beginning of this journey.

Now, on to the best publishing team in the history of publishing. Natalie Doherty, I absolutely love working with you and learned so much from you on *The Christmasaurus*, then somehow forgot it all and learned it all over again on this one! Your ideas are always spot on. Sorry if I'm a bit of a grumpypants sometimes! Francesca Dow, I'm so honored to call Penguin Random

ACKNOWLEDGEMENTS

House my publishing home—thanks for opening the door! Amanda Punter, thanks so much for believing in me and everything we do from books and beyond. Tom Weldon, I still can't quite believe you let me write books . . . Please never change your mind.

From brilliant editorial ideas to making the book look and feel so wonderful and SO much more, the following bunch of grown-ups all deserve a whole slop of thanks: Anthea Townsend, Hannah Bourne, Lauren Hyett, Rosamund Hutchinson, Andrea Bowie, Mandy Norman, Eliza Walsh, Wendy Shakespeare, Jane Tait, Sarah Roscoe, Anna Billson, Emily Smyth, Zosia Knopp, Camilla Borthwick, Maeve Banham, Susanne Evans, Nicola O'Connell, and Ceri Cooper.

I want to apologize to a few people for being a silly sausage and completely forgetting to thank them in *The Christmasaurus*: Tommy J. Smith, Nikki Garner, Simon Jones, and Kaz Gill. You all do SO much for me, from basically organizing my life to creating Christmas in July at the drop of a hat. Thanks to you all for your hard work—I hope you know how much it means to me.

That brings me to the fam. Giovanna, thanks for

supporting me in all that I do, for putting up with everything about me, and for letting me sleep with a light on. I've been waiting to write an appropriate book to dedicate to you, but seeing as I only seem to write about pooping dinosaurs or disgusting monsters, I guess this one will have to do! I love you. To my own two Creakers, Buzz and Buddy, you are the reason for all that I do—now go to bed! To Mom and Dad, thanks for showing me scary things as a kid. It's about time I turned the sleepless nights into something creative! Carrie, you like weird stuff and smell funny, so in many ways you're quite similar to a Creaker. X

Thanks to Danny, Dougie, and Harry for being equal parts of the best thing that ever happened to me, and I look forward to the day I'm standing onstage with you all again.

Finally, thanks to all the people who have supported me from the earliest days of McFly through to now. I've loved sharing music, books, and bits of my life with you and can't thank you enough for everything you do that gives me the opportunity to do everything that I do. You're all awesome.

Nothing is ordinary in the North Pole.

Turn the page for a peek at Tom Fletcher's
original story about a boy called William Trundle,
Santa's elves, and a most unusual dinosaur.

CHAPTER ONE

WILLIAM TRUNDLE

This is William Trundle.

There's something you should know about William: William liked dinosaurs. Actually, he didn't just like them. He *loved* them. In fact, he loved them so much I should probably write it in big letters like this:

WILLIAM LOVED DINOSAURS!

WILLIAM HAD . . . sorry,

William had dinosaur pajamas, dinosaur socks, dinosaur pants, a dinosaur-shaped toothbrush, dinosaur wallpaper, two dinosaur posters, a dinosaur lampshade, and more dinosaur toys than he could fit into a bag for life. But if there was one thing William knew for sure, it was that you could never have too many dinosaur toys!

William lived in a wonky little house on the edge of a busy town on the edge of a busier city, but even though the house was small, it never really felt that way, because only two people lived in it: William and his dad, Bob Trundle.

Now, I bet you're wondering why William didn't have a mom. Well, of course he did have a mom once, but sadly she died a long time ago, when William was very young. So it had been just William and Mr. Trundle for as long as William could remember.

As well as dinosaurs, William loved **Christmas**— but not half as much as his dad did.

Mr. Trundle loved Christmas so much that whenever Christmas Day was over, he would sob uncontrollably for a whole week, sometimes until the end of January, desperately clinging to Christmas! He even had a secret Christmas tree hidden in his closet. The tree was permanently decorated, and it lit up when he opened the door to get his clothes. Each morning as Mr. Trundle got dressed, he would look at his secret tree and say to himself, "Each day we move away from last Christmas is one day closer to the next." It was these words that got him through the year.

On this particular morning, though, Mr. Trundle was feeling very merry indeed—because it was the first day of December.

"Time to get ready for school, Willypoos!" Mr. Trundle called from the kitchen as he spread butter on two steaming-hot crumpets (Mr. Trundle's favorite breakfast).

William rolled his eyes at the silly nickname his dad used for him—*Willypoos*!

"Dad, you can't keep calling me that. I'm seven and three-quarters. It's embarrassing!" William shouted from his bedroom as he stuffed his schoolbag full of books.

"I thought we'd agreed that I can call you Willypoos when you're not at school? You can't go changing the rules willy-nilly, Willypoos!" Mr. Trundle teased as he walked into his son's bedroom. "Happy first of December!"

Mr. Trundle beamed as he placed a breakfast tray down on William's desk and nodded his head excitedly at a rectangular object perched perfectly next to the plate of golden crumpets. William followed his gaze and saw that it was a chocolate-filled Advent calendar.

"Thanks, Dad! Where's yours?" asked William. Every year, William and Mr. Trundle would each have an Advent calendar and open a new door together every morning before school. It was a Trundle tradition.

William thought he saw a flicker of sadness on Mr. Trundle's face, which was quickly replaced by a smile.

"I thought it might be fun to share one this year, William," Mr. Trundle said. Lately they'd been sharing a lot of things, as Mr. Trundle didn't have very much money. But William didn't mind.

"Oh, OK!" he said. "I'll open the door and you can have the first chocolate, Dad."

"How about *I* open the door and *you* have the first chocolate, William?" Mr. Trundle suggested.

"Thanks, Dad," William said, grinning. He'd secretly hoped his dad would say that.

"Say 'Cheese'!" said Mr. Trundle as he quickly snapped a photo of the two of them. "Ah, that'll make a lovely Christmas card this year!" he said, admiring the photograph. It was another Trundle tradition to take a photograph on the first of December for the Christmas cards they would send to a long list of their distant relatives: Aunty Kim on the Isle of Wight; Great-Nana Joan, who looked like a witch; cousins Lilly and Joe; Aunty Julie; second cousin Sam; Uncle H. Trundle; Great-Grandpa Ken. . . . It was a long list, half of whom William had never met!

"William, have you thought about what you're going to ask Santa for this year? You'll need to write your letter soon," said Mr. Trundle as he peeled open the first door on the Advent calendar. William took out the small snowman-shaped chocolate, but suddenly he didn't feel like eating it.

"My dear boy, what on earth's the matter?" asked Mr. Trundle.

"Well . . . it's . . . it's just that I don't think Santa can bring me what I want this year," said William, staring longingly at the dinosaur poster on his wall. "I'm pretty sure the elves can't make real dinosaurs."

"Make?" repeated Mr. Trundle as he took a knowing sip of his cup of tea. "The elves don't *make* anything at all!"

William looked very confused. "But I thought Santa's elves *made* all the presents at the North Pole," he said.

"Pah!" cried Mr. Trundle, spitting out a mouthful of tea. "Well, William, I'm afraid that's all just a big pile of poppycock, fiddle-faddle, mouth-waffling, gibbery-faff nonsense. Whoever told you that is a complete knobblyplank! *Make* presents? Ha! Would you like me to tell you how elves *really* work, William?" he asked, a sudden sparkle in his eyes.

"Oh, please do, Dad!" William cried, and made himself comfortable. He always loved it when his dad told him stories. Mr. Trundle was very good at them—and he was particularly good at Christmas stories, for, as you already know, he loved everything about Christmas.

ABOUT THE AUTHOR

Tom Fletcher is also the author of *The Christmasaurus, There's a Monster in Your Book, There's a Dragon in Your Book,* and with his wife, Giovanna Fletcher, *Eve of Man.* He is one of the UK's bestselling authors for children, and his books have been translated into more than thirty languages. He has never seen a Creaker in real life, but he's always keeping a close lookout.

@Tom Fletcher